Human Test

Book Two of the AI Diaries

Human Test

Foner Books

ISBN 978-1-948691-15-4

Copyright 2018 by E. M. Foner

Northampton, Massachusetts

One

"You're cut off, Hosea," I told my remaining customer when he pushed forward his empty tankard with a self-satisfied belch. "I'm not going to be responsible for you getting into an accident."

"Tor drives himself," the farmer protested, "and at the speed he goes, you'd have to be asleep in the road to get run over."

"And you've never slept in the road? Be honest, now."

Hosea opened his mouth and then closed it again, and I could practically see the neurons firing in his brain as he dredged up old memories. His shoulders slumped in defeat.

"Early to bed, early to rise," I consoled the disappointed man while presenting the slate with his tally. "That's thirty coppers worth you took onboard tonight, plus twenty-four more treating Yitzhak and Xeres after you beat them."

The memory of that triumph over his fellow date-growers immediately cheered Hosea. "My load weighed in four Kav more than Yitzhak's, and Xeres fell a full Se'ah short. That's from the same number of trees, mind you. It's all in the pollination technique." Here he performed a few intricate hand maneuvers that meant nothing to me. "If you figure thirty-three dates per Log, I beat them by…" he reached for the slate and looked around for a piece of chalk.

"You beat Yitzhak by five hundred and twenty-eight dates and Xeres by seven hundred and ninety-two," I provided the answer to speed him along his way.

Hosea's eye took on a peculiar gleam and he asked, "Can you break a gold?"

"You always do this to me," I complained. "No, I can't break a gold at the end of the night on a Weighing Day. I'm lucky if I can break a silver."

"Well, you'll just have to chalk it up to my account and I'll take care of it next time I'm here." He lurched up from his stool, planning a quick exit, but stumbled over a chair and almost ended up on the floor before catching his balance. "Excuse me," Hosea said to the chair in that strange version of Aramaic that was spoken by the inhabitants. The language also included large vocabulary borrowings from Classical Greek and other Mediterranean tongues, the region of Earth from which the Ferrymen had originally drawn the population for this continent of the world.

"Maybe you'd better sleep it off in the storeroom," I suggested. "I'll set up the bunk."

"Tor will bring the wagon home," he insisted, then reversed course and headed for the restroom. "I'll just leave my contribution to the tannery in the old barrel. You ought to give your customers a discount for all of the urea you get out of us."

"It's a recycling service, Dan doesn't pay me," I called after Hosea, who didn't respond. "Alright, then. I'll just get your team turned around."

There were two oxen yoked to the farm cart, but Tor was the older and wiser of the pair, and more curious as well. He and his companion were finished with the grain Hosea had poured into the feed trough for them before

2

entering my establishment, and Tor may have thought that their master had sent me out with dessert. Hope springs eternal in draft animals, but it wasn't to be.

"Back," I called to the oxen, strongly enough to get their attention, but hopefully not so loud as to wake eBeth, who was asleep upstairs by this hour. I was never one to hit animals, not even thick-skinned ones that barely noticed the driver's goad, but I let a little electricity flow through the hand I put on the younger ox's flank to let him know I meant business. A couple more "Backs" and a "Haw" later, and I had the team and the wagon pointed down the road in the direction of Hosea's home.

"Thanks," the farmer said, climbing up on the bench. Then he leaned towards me, coming perilously close to an unintended descent, and asked in a loud stage whisper, "Want to see something?"

"Are you sure you aren't going to fall off that seat? It must be a good half-hour drive to your place."

"That's what I want to show you," he said, his face taking on a crafty look. "See this harness?" he demanded, holding up a confused tangle of leather straps.

"Are you thinking of replacing your oxen with horses or mules?" I asked in surprise.

"It's not for the animals." He hiccupped and squirmed his way into the restraints, which I now saw were tied through hooks on the bench and the wagon body. "Your cousin Paul made it for me special." After tightening a strap across his chest, he threw himself violently from side to side, and sure enough, the harness kept his body firmly upright and in place. "No more falling off the wagon for me. Get up! Get up, there!" he cried, and the two oxen began their walk home.

"Wouldn't hurt you to spend some time on the wagon for real," I called after him, knowing that he wouldn't understand my reference even if he heard me.

In the six months since we arrived on Reservation, I've noted that the humans are surprisingly moderate in their alcohol consumption compared to their counterparts back on Earth, but Hosea had been hitting it a bit hard since his wife moved away. She left him a note saying that after thirty years of farming the same patch of land she wanted to see the ocean, but Sue tells me it's more complicated than that.

Back inside, I snuffed all but one of the candles to save on wax and began quietly straightening up in the dim light. A ghostly figure appeared on the stairs leading down from the second floor. It was eBeth in her nightshirt.

"Who was that shouting at the oxen?" she asked in a sleepy voice.

"Hosea. He's been having a hard time lately. Have you seen Spot?"

"He's sleeping on my bed. I tried to send him down to check on the noise but he just yawned at me and started that fake snoring he does to get out of moving his lazy butt."

"You have school in the morning and you're a growing girl," I reminded her. "You should be getting your rest."

"And you should have cut off Hosea two ales ago," she retorted. "Anyway, I've been having problems in class and Sue suggested that I talk to you."

"I'm sure she meant in the morning," I said, but eBeth had already slumped into a chair. I took the seat opposite while cursing the idiot who had decided that the team should maintain radio frequency silence, which prevented me from contacting Sue to find out what was on the girl's mind. "Is it about boys?"

"What's wrong with you?" she demanded, coming fully awake. "How come every time a woman has a problem, whatever man she tells about it just assumes that it's some other man? Death Lord asked the same question."

"You agreed to call Peter by his given name while we're here. Death Lord carries a certain negative connotation amongst primitive cultures."

"If you think this society is primitive then our culture back on Earth must have struck you as positively prehistoric," she shot back, and paused for me to contradict her. I let the opportunity pass in silence, so she continued with, "I feel like I'm deceiving them."

"Technically, you are deceiving them, but that doesn't change anything," I told her. "Learning a new language is good for human brain development, and they can always speak it with each other."

"But the school hired me to teach the children Northern! What if they find out?"

"How? By traveling a month to the coast, booking passage on one of the three trading fleets a year that makes the long voyage to the northern continent when the winds are right, and then coming back here and telling everybody? If one of your students left tomorrow, I doubt they could complete the round trip in a year, and by then we'll be finished here."

"But I'm teaching them English!" eBeth persisted as if I hadn't said anything. "They'll be the only ones within a million light years who can speak it."

"Our galaxy isn't even a hundred thousand light years across—" I began, but she must not have been in the mood for a math lesson because she talked right over my explanation.

"And it's not just children. Some of the kids who are auditing the class are my age, and the headmaster has been sitting in with some other old people. He even asked if I would be interested in teaching a night class for adults."

"That's quite a compliment, but I don't want you stretching yourself too thin," I told her seriously. "You could give up being my apprentice, of course, but I thought you enjoyed learning about state-of-the-art technology."

"Don't make fun of these people. It's not their fault that electrical generation and internal combustion engines are banned. I doubt any of them have even seen the authenticity videos for the products that they're making. They just stand in front of the lens on those little cubes they call "Ferrymen's Eyes' and talk about their work."

"I'm using the term in a local context. Gears and hydraulics are state-of-the-art on this world and I happen to find them fascinating. Maintaining complex machinery is also the ideal cover job since it gives me an excuse to travel to the surrounding villages and towns."

"But my students trust me and I'm lying to them," eBeth practically wailed.

"You knew we would be undercover when you signed on for the mission," I reminded her. "When I was running my computer repair service and restaurant training school back on Earth, did I run around admitting to people that I was an alien artificial intelligence construct?"

"Sometimes, when you were recruiting labor for off-world jobs. Besides, you and your team acted so weird that anybody who was paying attention could have guessed."

"Do your students enjoy the class?"

"That just makes me feel more guilty. I've even heard people who aren't my students using English words at the market, like the kids are bringing it home. The worst part is that I'm not getting any more fluent in Modern Aramaic, or whatever you decided to call it."

"You're progressing just fine," I assured her. "It's typical for humans your age who are learning a new language in an immersive environment to make their biggest gains in the first few months. Your progress is slowing now because you can communicate pretty well with what you've already learned."

"Death Lord speaks it better than I do."

"Peter is interacting with customers at Paul's machine shop all day, while you're teaching English in the mornings and working with me in the afternoons. I could start speaking to you exclusively in the local—"

"No," she interrupted hastily. "I have enough trouble understanding you when I know all the words you're using. Sue is a saint for putting up with you."

"Speaking of my second-in-command, have you seen her tonight?"

"She said something about her weaving circle getting near the end of their carpet, so the women are staying late this week. It's almost the holidays and they're all counting on the extra income."

"What is it, eBeth?" I asked, catching the troubled note in her voice.

"Why do these people celebrate Ferrymen's Day?"

"To commemorate being moved to this world."

"You see," the girl said in frustration. "This is exactly what I mean. We're speaking the same language but we aren't communicating."

I could have admitted that she was right, but instead I took a stab in the dark. "Did you mean to ask why these people are happy that the Ferrymen took them from Earth and brought them here in the first place?"

"Obviously. And why the people aren't angry that the Ferrymen prohibit them from developing modern technology. Do you know what one of the other teachers said when I asked her about textbooks?"

"I wasn't there and you didn't tell me about it."

"It was a rhetorical question. She told me that movable type was all well and fine for reference books, but that the students learn better when they pay attention to the teachers and take notes. It's like they're collaborating with their captors!"

"After six months on Reservation, you still think of the Ferrymen as kidnappers?" I asked in surprise. "That's never been the way they operated. All of these people, or their ancestors, chose to board the landing craft and make the interstellar journey."

"But they thought they were obeying the will of the Sky Gods."

"I don't think that's the case. It's true that primitive people often mistake advanced aliens for gods, but that doesn't mean there's malicious intent involved."

"How can posing as gods not be malicious?"

"The Ferrymen are members of the League of Sentient Entities Regulating Space," I pointed out. "I won't bore you with all the case law about Sky God procedures, but it boils down to efficiency. Imagine it's a few thousand years ago on Earth and there's been a natural disaster like a drought, or that an army has just marched through and seized all of the livestock and food stores, including seeds for the next year's crop. A transport drops from the heavens, an emissary invites the survivors to move to a world without wars, and the offer includes feeding and sheltering the people until they can get back on their feet."

"Plus accepting their rescuers as gods and being exploited to make hand-crafted goods for the galactic luxury market," eBeth interjected.

"All of that comes much later, when the population is established. You've seen the stone tablets in front of the village temple. They're a copy of the legal covenant between the Ferrymen and the humans."

"Sounds like a religion to me."

"A covenant is just another word for a contract. And if you read it, you'll note that there's nothing in there about worship, sacrifices, or cheap labor."

"But the Ferrymen treat this whole planet like a factory," eBeth argued, the indignation rising in her voice. "Maybe Sue enjoys tying little knots in carpets and recording all the weaving songs for your cultural archives, but the women who live here don't have a choice."

"What makes you say that?" I asked, sincerely puzzled by the question. "It's true that we're here to investigate the conditions and report back to Library's representative on the League's executive council, but I haven't seen anything yet that would be considered a violation."

"The Ferrymen are keeping these people from advancing!"

"They placed certain restrictions on industrialization but that's just their version of social engineering. If the people weren't happy, the Ferrymen wouldn't get their Persian carpets and dragon saddles for export. I think it's a synergistic relationship."

"Parasitic."

"Go to sleep, eBeth. We can talk about this tomorrow—I mean, later today if you like."

"I'm going up because I'm tired and I have to teach in the morning, not because you're right, which you aren't," she told me, rising from the chair. "And you shouldn't keep serving Hosea until he can barely sit on his wagon."

I thought briefly about protesting, but the truth was I already felt guilty about selling Hosea that last ale, and maybe the one before it. The fact he hadn't paid me took the sting off my conscience, and I went back to putting the chairs up on the tables so I could sweep the floor. Frenay would mop when she came in the morning to help her husband with the cooking. When I purchased The Eatery from the couple who had previously owned it, they had agreed to stay on for one year in return for my paying the carpenter who was building their vacation cottage on the lake.

"Guess who," somebody called from the doorway.

I spun around at the unfamiliar voice, but it was just Sue imitating one of the women from her weaving circle.

"I wish you would stop doing that," I grumbled as my second-in-command came up and gave me a kiss on the cheek. She pulled away with a hurt expression, and I immediately corrected myself. "Not the kissing, the impersonations. I'm jumpy enough going around with all of my active sensors shut down. I understand that kissing is important to you as a sign of our deepening relationship."

"Whose idiotic idea was it to enforce radio frequency silence?"

"Mine," I admitted. "We don't know whether the Ferrymen are monitoring the spectrum for alien visitors or violations in their covenant so we have to avoid using any advanced technology."

"Except for the antenna array you have Paul building to watch for Pffift's arrival."

"It's all passive, except for the receiver, and that's so well shielded that you wouldn't notice the emissions if you were standing right on top of it. If I didn't give Paul something constructive to work on he'd just end up making trouble. Besides, I gave Pffift my word."

"He doesn't seem to be in any hurry to come see us," Sue said, stroking the artificial hair on the back of my encounter suit's arm as if I was one of her cats. "We almost finished the carpet for that T'poulf merchant prince, though it's beyond me why he'd want visitors walking on a giant portrait of himself."

"What do the other women in your weaving circle think of it?"

"Ruth thought he was kind of cute for a Pegasus-looking species, but she was the only one to express an opinion. To the rest of our circle, it's just some image delivered by the purchasing agent to be replicated on a carpet. From what they tell me, the business model hasn't changed in the dozen generations since this world started accepting special orders from the Ferrymen in addition to making their usual products. The women look forward to their weaving nights as a chance to get out of the house, come into the village center, and trade juicy gossip. Do you want to know what they think about Justin and Kim?"

"Have those two blown their cover already?"

"As apothecaries? No, just the married part. Cybele swears that her cousin from the provincial capital got the true story from a medicinal herb distributor. According to her, Justin ran out on his wife and children after falling in love with his apprentice."

"So who is Kim supposed to be?"

Sue pulled away and looked at me like I had rocks in my head.

"Justin's former apprentice?" I hazarded a guess.

"Sometimes I think you're finally beginning to get it," my second-in-command said, giving me a quick hug. "I'll be upstairs working on my report and spending some quality time with my cats. Did I tell you they're both expecting?"

"Kittens, right?" Six months of living in the same house with Sue and eBeth had taught me that it was easier to cover up my social deficiencies if they thought I was joking all of the time.

Even before she finished her perfunctory laugh, I graded my interactions for the last twenty minutes and gave myself an internal pat on the back. The two correct guesses had put me over fifty percent in my conversations with Sue and eBeth since arriving on Reservation, and the second derivative showed that my accuracy was increasing. It was only a matter of time now before the women in my life stopped treating me like the village idiot.

Two

"You're trying to sell me something, aren't you, Mark?" Sophus asked suspiciously. "Whenever you start talking about efficiency, I feel the urge to hide my wallet."

"I just want to make your life easier," I protested. "The calculator is free. I'm taking them around to all of the millers in the area."

"Including Cleo?" Sophus and his brother, Cleo, had fallen out over business differences after the death of their father and were now rivals.

"No, and if you'd just look at the calculator you'd see why. It's strictly for waterwheels. Your brother runs a windmill."

"Ought to be a law against those things," Sophus grumbled. "My niece lives a five-minute walk from that eyesore her father built and she swears she can hear it squeaking in her sleep."

I made a mental note to order more lubricant from the supplier and shoved the custom slide rule into the miller's calloused hand.

"You won't have to guess at the sluice gate heights anymore," I told him. "You just set the cursor on the top scale to the flow rate and read off the millstone RPMs on the bottom scale. It couldn't be simpler."

"The moving glass piece with the line on it is the cursor?" he asked. "I've seen my daughter using something like this for the astronomy homework she brings home from the academy on vacation. So what's the purpose of the sliding scale in the middle?"

"That gives you the expected yield in flour based on the crop," I told him. "Plus, if you're grinding on shares rather than charging per weight, you can figure out your profit ahead of time."

"So this row of digits on the slider is the number of bags of grain?" He tapped it with a thick fingernail.

"I did it as weight since the bag size isn't as standard as you might think. The top line on the slider is for wheat, the one below it is corn, and the next one is barley. The bottom line is your profit in coppers."

"It's a lot of numbers," he complained, but I could see he was intrigued by the operation, and I stood by silently as he worked through a couple of calculations based on orders he'd recently filled. "I guess it might save me a little time," Sophus finally allowed. "How much?"

"It's a gift."

The miller shoved the slide rule back in my hand. "Beware of Greeks bearing gifts," he proclaimed, reminding me again that some of the ancestors of the local population had been transplanted from Earth less than two thousand years ago.

"Between the two of us, you're the one with the Greek name, and I'll make my money when you call me for repairs. The calculator is part of my new advertising campaign."

Sophus looked at the slide rule again, and this time he read off the branding, "Mark's Mechanical Repairs and Custom Engineering Solutions. The Eatery, Covered Bridge, Fourth Province, 8GJX-4D."

14

"There's a free case to keep the dust out," I added, handing him a leather sleeve with the same branding stamped in gilt.

"I'm afraid you made a mistake with the new postal code," he informed me. "We're 4F."

"That's because you're on the other side of the Weir River," I told him. "The Village of Covered Bridge is 4D, and Old Bridge is 4E."

"I'll never get used to the new system," Sophus complained. "If it wasn't for the pre-punched postage I wouldn't use it at all. How can a few little holes in a scrap of stiff paper stuck to the edge of the envelope make it easier to deliver the mail?"

"You must have seen the punch cards some of the mechanical looms use to repeat standard patterns. It's the same principle, except the postal service uses the holes to mechanically sort the letters without somebody having to read every address. Simon showed me a gelatin silver print of the main sorting room at the provincial capital. They handle hundreds of thousands of letters a day."

"Where do they get the power to do that? Windmills?"

"They have a take-off wheel on the aqueduct and overhead belts on the sorting floor, just like a machine shop powered by a dam. People in the capital have been complaining for hundreds of years that their water pressure was too high, so the department of public works killed two birds with one stone."

"I'll let you know how this works out," Sophus said, setting the slide rule on the high shelf behind the large scale. "So you rode all the way out here just to give me this?"

"Sue told me that your wife was having a problem with her sewing machine. They're in the same weaving circle."

"What are you getting for Ferrymen's Day?" he asked, suddenly sounding like a small boy.

"Whatever Sue sees fit to give me," I replied, in keeping with my cover. The inhabitants of Covered Bridge believe that Sue and I are married and that eBeth is our daughter. The last thing I wanted was to make a slip that would have the whole village gossiping about us like Justin and Kim. "I wouldn't mind a new saddle for my bicycle."

"I'm getting a telescope," he said. "A reflector, so I can keep up with what Athena is learning in academy." He put his hands together with the fingers intermeshed and held his arms out from his body in a hoop. "The mirror is going to be this big."

"That's the size of the reflector at the observatory in Springfield," I said, naming the nearby academy town, "but whatever it is, let me know if you need help setting it up. My niece is an expert."

"Helen? No offense, Mark, but I don't know if I want that woman around my daughter. Word is that she's a bit fast."

"Only on her bicycle, Sophus. Now I'd better stop inside and see your better half before she sends Sue a note with your messenger dog asking where I am. I don't want to end up with a lump of coal for my Ferrymen's Day gift."

The miller chuckled at my open admission of who ruled the roost. "What are you giving your wife?" he asked as I was leaving.

"Still shopping," I replied with a vague hand wave, though his question gave me pause. Was Sue expecting me to give her a Ferrymen's Day present? I made a mental note to check with eBeth.

The miller's messenger dog greeted me with a tail thump as I took the short path from the mill to the cottage.

Mercurys, or "Go, Boys," as they were familiarly known, had been bred on Reservation to carry messages and small packages in the unending rural sprawl of small farms and hamlets. A trained Mercury could remember a hundred or more specific locations or individuals by name. The Eatery had a thriving takeout business at lunchtime, the messenger dogs showing up with orders and coins and returning to their masters with the food in saddlebags.

"Come in, Mark," Palti greeted me at the door of the large post-and-beam cottage. "I just made cookies. Sue tells me that you're a big fan of oatmeal-raisin."

"That's right," I lied, raisins being a particular problem for my encounter suit since they tended to swell in the holding tank and stick to the walls unless I run an extra flush cycle. "I always wondered what you ladies talked about while knotting rugs and now I guess I know."

"She's very proud of you and your daughter. We've never had a clockmaker living in the village before, and when you finish training eBeth, we'll have two."

"Sue told me there's a problem with your sewing machine," I said, taking three warm cookies from the proffered plate in a demonstration of enthusiasm. When Palti turned her back to set the plate on her side table, I slipped one of the cookies in my pocket and declared, "Tasty." The miller's wife smiled at me over her shoulder as I made appreciative chewing motions.

"The treadle doesn't move," she summed up the sewing machine's problem. "I asked Sophus to look at it, but he's only good with equipment that weighs at least as much as he does, and Athena is more of a theoretician."

"Did she offer a hypothesis?"

"Does 'I think something is jammed' count?"

"That's a reasonable guess. Why don't we have a look?"
As soon as she turned her back, I slipped a second cookie
into my pocket. I'd have to remember to take them out for
eBeth or I'd end up with Spot's slobber and crumbs in there
when he sniffed them out.

Palti led me to the old treadle sewing machine that she
had inherited from her mother, who had no doubt received
it from her own mother and so on for a number of generations. The basic technology was frozen in time due to the
Ferrymen's prohibition on electrical generation, but the
foot-powered design was an elegant engineering solution,
and like vintage machines on Earth, the iron scrollwork
that supported the table made an artistic statement that is
so often missing from later industrial periods.

Treadles are widely used on Reservation when water or
wind power isn't practical, especially for the small machines like wood lathes and grindstones that are so
common in cottage-based production. In addition to
subsistence farming, most of the landowners in the area
sell their excess or raise a specialty crop for export to
nearby towns or transport by barge to the capital city via
the network of canals that has been developed over thousands of years. The majority of farm families also practice
one or more crafts to supplement their income, selling
wooden bowls, leather-work, and other items to the
Ferrymen for export off-world.

"Athena's hypothesis was spot on," I told Palti, who
beamed proudly at her daughter's acumen. "It's not in the
treadle mechanism or I'd see the jam right off. I'll have to
check the transmission."

"Take all the time you need. I'm making another batch
of cookies so you can take them home with you."

"Thanks," I said, and as soon as she left, I slipped the final cookie into my pocket. As in most homes, the crafting room had the best natural sunlight, provided by large windows with dozens of panes of bulls-eye glass. I quickly located the problem, a buildup of lint holding a fragment of broken needle in just the wrong place where it jammed the gears, and I was able to finesse it out without even returning to my bicycle for the tool kit. Sometimes my encounter suit's ability to blow air like a compressor really comes in handy. I pumped the treadle a few times and nodded in satisfaction.

"Don't tell me you need to mail-order parts," Palti begged when I returned to the kitchen much sooner than she expected. "Couldn't your friend Paul make whatever's necessary? I'm willing to pay a bit more to save a couple of weeks."

"No parts required," I told her. "You're all set."

"You really are as talented as your wife is always telling us," Palti said, and for a moment, I wondered if I'd detected a subtle criticism of Sue's one-woman admiration society in the compliment. "How much do I owe you?"

"The cookies are pay enough," I told her. "Besides, I needed an excuse to stop by and see your husband, but I do have to be getting back to the village now."

"I thought you only worked nights in The Eatery."

"Yes, but the school's headmaster wants to see me, and I'll use the opportunity to look in on eBeth's class."

"You know, nobody would ever take you for foreigners," Palti said, handing me a paper sack of cookies. "If it wasn't for eBeth and Paul's apprentice not speaking the language when you all arrived, we would have thought you were just moving from the next province over."

"That's because eBeth and Peter grew up on the northern continent after we were shipwrecked," I fibbed, in accordance with our cover story. "The rest of us were born and bred in Province Eleven, and though it's a long way from here, life is pretty much the same."

I wheeled my eight-speed bike out of the miller's yard, hopped onto the narrow saddle, and began pedaling down the long drive to the aptly named Miller's Road. The sound of a baying hound and a tan streak cutting through the extensive vegetable garden informed me that I was engaged in a race. Unfortunately, the messenger dog had chosen the right angle, and even though I pumped as hard as I could without breaking traction or risking damage to the bike, he intercepted me just as I turned onto the road.

For a few seconds I tried to ignore the dog's frantic barking and the dramatic snaps, but finally I was compelled to give in and pay his tithe. The Mercury, who had been tortured by the smell of baking all morning, caught the oatmeal-raisin cookie neatly in his mouth and skidded to a halt to enjoy the fruits of his efforts. Like many of the dogs living at local farms, he was a washout from the postal service's Mercury training school, and I suspected that it was his predilection for chasing bicycles that cost him a shot at a civil service job.

Miller's Road ran directly into Provincial Highway 73, which was the east-west road that also served as the main street for Covered Bridge. Like most rural highways off the main trading routes, it was a dirt road that could get pretty messy in the rain, but there wasn't enough traffic to justify an upgrade. The main commercial arteries running between provinces were two-lane stone roads that would have made the Romans jealous, and the tow roads running alongside the canal network were generally "improved," depending on the local conditions.

"Where's the fire?" an older rider called to me as I shot past at more than double the speed he was making.

"Just doing a little sprint to test a repair," I called back, braking at the same time to allow him to catch up. Saul was plugged into the provincial government through his job as the county safety inspector and not a person I wanted taking an interest in my actions.

"I heard the miller's dog barking so I wasn't surprised," he said with a chuckle. "Did you buy him off?"

"I gave him a cookie," I said with a nod. "What brings you all the way out here this morning?"

"Cyrus has his sheep in the high pasture and he reported seeing something funny at the last triple moon. Can you think of any reason a person would be out on the mountain digging holes at night?"

Unfortunately, the reason that immediately came to mind was Paul burying pop-up masts for the antenna array, but I wasn't going to share my suspicion with Saul.

"Planting something?" I suggested.

"Wrong season, wrong dirt, wrong altitude," Saul replied, giving me a sidelong glance with his sharp hazel eyes. "Try again?"

"Mining for gold? I've heard that a man could make a living panning some of those streams running down the Twelve Sisters into our valley."

"In the dark?" he asked skeptically.

"You said it was a triple moon," I pointed out. "Besides, Old Cyrus is half-blind, so if he thought he saw somebody digging, there must have been enough light to work. Assuming it wasn't one of the Originals."

"And that's why I'm going out to check," the inspector said. "We don't get too many of the natives this far west, but there have been an unusual number of sightings in the area lately, and it's part of my job to make sure that nobody interferes with them. It's funny that the Ferrymen are so protective of the Originals, but who knows the minds of Sky Gods."

I knew exactly why the humans on Reservation were forbidden from directly interfering with the Originals but I couldn't explain to the inspector that the Ferrymen were playing by the League's rules. There was no prohibition against colonizing sparsely occupied planets, even though it was taken for granted that this would interfere with the natural development of primitive natives, but intentional interactions were still subject to regulation.

"Are you familiar with the history of our first contact?" he continued.

"Just what I know from school," I offered the expected answer.

"When the Ferrymen first brought us to Reservation and gave us the covenant, they explained that we were welcome here as permanent guests, but the world was already occupied. Our ancestors were introduced to the Originals, but the natives didn't have the capacity for language, at least, not spoken language. The safety inspectors do a rough census of Originals every ten years, but their numbers appear to be stable."

"And low."

"Barely enough for a breeding population, I'd think, not that anybody has ever reported seeing any offspring. But the Ferrymen banned our scholars from studying the Originals and we train our children to walk away if they ever encounter one."

"It's not a bad compromise for two species sharing the same planet," I said. "There's no overlap between your food sources, and the natives are solitary night foragers who prefer the hills and swamps. I haven't seen any evidence that the Originals are frightened of humans and I'm sure they would find a way to express their complaints if there was any serious friction. Their cliff-art and food preservation techniques display higher cognitive functions."

"No, there's no overlap between our food sources," Saul said, and his emphasis on 'our' made me aware of my earlier verbal slip. "You seem to have more interest in the subject than most people."

"Here's my turn," I declared, veering towards the bridle path that led the back way to the school. "I hope you stop by The Eatery on your way home. I won't be there because I've got a repair in Old Furnace this afternoon, but tell them I said it's on the house."

I didn't look back to see how Saul took my sudden departure, and I put on a burst of speed just to make sure he wouldn't follow to continue his new line of questioning. Something about the county safety inspector always made me feel like he knew more than he was letting on.

Three

The morning session was nearing an end when I reached the village school. As adjunct faculty without a homeroom, eBeth taught in the auditorium where the village meetings were also held. All of the large-capacity rooms on Reservation that I'd visited featured a lush indoor garden in the back which may have been intended as a natural air purifier. At first glance, I wondered if the entire student body was in attendance, and I felt guilty about having pushed eBeth to accept the job shortly after we arrived. Then I realized that the audience was divided into three distinct groups, and only the twenty or so youngsters at the front were official students.

Behind the children sat a similar number of teenagers, most of them a year or two younger than eBeth, an age where the teens remaining in the village were typically working as apprentices or in a family business. Further back sat a thinly spread group of adults, including the headmaster, two members of the village council, and a few people I didn't recognize.

"Who wants to try reading today's tongue twister?" eBeth asked her students in English while tapping the blackboard with a long pointer. "Yes, Naomi?"

"Peter Piper picked a peck of pickled peppers," the girl reeled off proudly.

"Excellent," eBeth congratulated her. "Are there any questions about today's class before we break for lunch?

My students only," she added when several adults raised their hands.

"What's a peck?" a boy asked.

"A Northern measure," eBeth told him. "It's like, a, uh, Log, only different."

"How do you pick pickled peppers?" a farm girl demanded. "You have to pick the peppers first and then pickle them."

"Who pickles peppers?" another child asked.

"It's not meant to be literal," eBeth explained, drawing blank stares from her class for using an unfamiliar word. "I mean, the point of a tongue twister is to improve your ability to speak clearly, not to convey, uh, deliver information."

At the base of the school's bell tower the designated student began energetically ringing the lunch hour. eBeth's class dissolved into a frenzied packing away of notebooks and a preliminary round of trading desserts before the main bartering event took place in the small cafeteria. The village school was the only stone structure in town, and the lack of recent additions testified to the relative stability of the local population. I watched as one of the departing students made a detour to the front of the class and shyly presented eBeth with an apple before fleeing after his fellows.

"Thank you for coming on such short notice, Mark," the headmaster addressed me from his seat as I navigated my way through the outbound flow of students.

"Joshua," I greeted him. "I'm surprised to find you in my daughter's class. If I had known there would be adults in attendance I would have negotiated a higher pay rate for her."

"You mean you would have tried," he replied, surprising me by responding in English. Then he ruined his show of fluency by adding, "I is a very good student, being."

"Yes you is," I told him, as I wasn't being paid to correct anybody's English. "I'm taking eBeth to Old Furnace on a clock repair job this afternoon. I hope you're not keeping her after school."

"No, no." He smiled crookedly at my weak joke and switched back to his native tongue. "It's actually a bit of council business. We all feel that it's time the village got its own turret clock and we'd like to hire you to purchase one for us."

"The school's bell tower doesn't have room," I cautioned him, though I was intrigued by the possibility of raising the roof, so to speak.

"It's for the steeple on the Ferrymen Temple," he told me.

"But nobody goes there," I said, calling up an image of the steeple from memory. Sure enough, the steeple had been designed with blank spots for a clock face on each of the four walls. Due to the temple's location on the highest land in the village, a clock would be visible for a good ways in every direction. "Does the council really have that kind of money to invest? A new turret clock costs as much as a dozen good bicycles."

"That's why we need you to buy us an old one and recondition it," the headmaster told me. "We'll compensate you for all of your time, of course."

"Of course," I grumbled, knowing that I would end up eating most of the hours for the sake of goodwill. But the truth is that I enjoy working on turret clocks, and taking one apart to the last screw and pin would make an interesting apprenticeship graduation project for eBeth. "What's your budget for the purchase?"

"We're still wrangling, but I thought, eight gold?" he ventured, a price that would be just about right for a single bicycle.

"It will take a while," I warned him. "There's a section of ads for used machines and such in the back pages of the Engineer's Journal but I don't remember seeing anything that would fit in your price range. Eight gold will limit us to clocks being sold for parts, but as long as the frame and the basic movement are intact, I can work with Paul to fabricate anything else that's needed."

"Are you sure you can't just build one from scratch?" the headmaster asked slyly.

"Sure he can," eBeth interjected, having taken advantage of my ban on active sensing to sneak up behind me. "That would be a great project for us."

"Paul doesn't have a foundry to cast the frame parts," I reminded her, "and the escapement requires precision machining."

"Whatever," eBeth said, knowing better than to get into an argument in front of the headmaster about the exact level of technological cheating I would permit myself and my team members.

"I'll let you know before I order anything so you can arrange for the payment," I told the headmaster.

"There's no need to be so formal," he said, standing up and gathering his notes. "Just buy what you think is best and put in for reimbursement. And thank you for an excellent class today, eBeth. It's wonderful how quickly the children are progressing."

The headmaster hurried off before I could protest the purchasing arrangement, leaving me with the distinct impression that I'd been hustled. The economy of Reservation was split between cash and barter, with the latter being more popular in the rural areas where coin wasn't as easy to come by. As a result, the inhabitants were well versed in deal-making.

"Let's go," eBeth said. "I packed a lunch."

"It's bad for your digestion to eat while pedaling, not to mention riding with no hands on these roads."

"I know. I'll eat when we get there. It's around ten miles, right?"

"Ninety stadia," I told her. "You should use the local units even when we're talking English so that they become second nature."

"Like I'm going to need to know a bunch of ancient Greek and Aramaic measures to get ahead in life," eBeth retorted. She pulled her bike out from the faculty rack and wheeled it alongside as we headed for the visitor rack, which in a reversal from the norm on Earth was the farthest parking area from the school entrance. "Why didn't they just choose one system or the other?"

"I suspect it was more of a natural process than a matter of choice. The number of individuals the Ferrymen transported was relatively low so it's quite likely that the different ethnic groups were forced to depend on each other for specialist knowledge. For example, if the Greeks supplied the road engineers, it would make sense that their units were adopted for longer lengths."

"It's worse than the metric system they tried to teach us in school," she complained as I retrieved my own bike. "None of the units make sense."

"People are always most comfortable using the system they grew up with. Take the calendar."

"Don't even get me started on the calendar," eBeth grunted, hopping on her bike and standing to put all of her weight on the left pedal. "I have to ask Sue to translate it just to figure out how old I really am."

I caught up with her at the gate and pointed in the direction of Old Furnace, which not surprisingly lay beyond Old Bridge. "Years are based on planetary orbits, it's the same around the galaxy," I told her. "The humans brought to this world stuck with a seven-day week even though Reservation's day is a good fifteen percent longer than Earth's. The year is just over three hundred days, which if you adjust for the planet's rotational speed, makes it about five percent shorter than an Earth year. It wouldn't have been that difficult for the ancestors of these people to become acclimated. The Ferrymen catalog large numbers of worlds in order to find the ones most suitable for their population transplant operations."

"If the day is fifteen percent longer, how come it still has twenty-four hours?"

"You can blame the ancient Egyptians for that one. I believe they started with a ten-hour day for sundials, added an hour to each end for dawn and dusk, and then doubled it for night."

"The math doesn't work," eBeth argued.

"The second here is longer than an Earth-second, making the minute longer as well. The relationship between the units is based on the Babylonian sexagesimal system, base sixty mathematics. It's how they ended up with sixty copper coins in a silver, and sixty silver coins in a gold."

"I thought that seconds were based on atomic clocks or something," eBeth argued. "You're saying that it's all relative."

"I'm saying it's all arbitrary. Advanced science allows civilizations to define their basic units with ever-increasing accuracy, but it's strictly a matter of mutual agreement."

We rode on in silence for a while, which gave eBeth a chance to digest the information dump. It must have come as a surprise to her that the seconds and minutes weren't the same here as on Earth, a fact I'd put off explaining from day to day on the advice of Sue, who claimed the girl already had enough adjustments to make. When we reached the main road and turned towards Old Furnace, eBeth must have finished processing the latest data, because she asked, "Why are bicycles so expensive here?"

"They're cheaper than automobiles on your world, and they last a lot longer with proper care."

"I'd have to save my whole salary from the school for the rest of the year to buy this bike."

"One of the perks of your job," I told her. "I'd be a poor master not to provide transportation for my apprentice."

We pedaled along in silence for a few short minutes, and then eBeth asked, "Where do ball bearings come from?"

"Do you mean that in the general sense, or are we still talking about the locally manufactured bicycles?"

"These ball bearings," she replied, pointing down at the crank as she pedaled.

"They're imported from other worlds. I've seen advertisements in the Engineer's Journal. Humans here could in principle manufacture ball bearings themselves, but hydraulic power and gear-driven control systems would produce an inferior product to what's cheaply available on the galactic market."

"That's what I thought," eBeth said, and I could tell from the tone of her voice that we were headed for yet another argument about Sky Gods exploiting gullible humans. "If the Ferrymen allowed us to generate electricity we could build better machines and factories and we wouldn't have to buy imported ball bearings that make bikes so expensive."

"Us?" I chided her.

"You know what I mean," she shot back. "How much of this bicycle originated off-world?"

"Just the ball bearings, eBeth, and at most they cost a handful of coppers. The bicycles are expensive because they aren't mass produced using robots. Paul could make a living turning out one bicycle a month if that was how he wanted to spend his time."

"You're telling me that somebody made this steel tubing in a little mill on a river?" she asked skeptically.

"The frame is heavier than bicycles sold on Earth because of the cruder manufacturing techniques available here," I pointed out. "There are some large factories in the provincial capitals that turn out steel tubing, rubber tires, and other basic components that are too inefficient to produce in a small shop."

"So the Ferrymen break their own rules when it suits them to keep the wheels of industry turning."

"The large factories run on water power, which is one of the reasons their use is limited to vital components. There are only so many prime locations to build dams or aqueducts."

"Why are you always defending them?" eBeth demanded. "Sometimes I suspect that you think humans are better off with alien overlords."

"I never said that," I protested. "I have less than four years of experience observing your people with over three years of that coming on Earth. But if I had to pick a place to raise a human child—"

"That's what I just said. You DO think we're better off here."

"According to Kim, these people are a lot healthier than Earthlings, mentally as well as physically. She hypothesizes that exercise has a great deal to do with it, but the lower levels of pollution and stress are also major factors."

"So maybe we should invite the Ferrymen to take over Earth and we can all start making handicrafts at home."

"Sarcasm is unattractive in a young lady, and it seems to me that quite a few humans were taking advantage of your Internet craft-store sites to do just that," I reminded her.

"I do miss the Internet," eBeth said, and if I were human I would have breathed a sigh of relief over successfully changing the subject. "Especially the gaming. One of the older kids in my class invited me to their game night and I'm thinking of going, just to see what it's like. She said they have role-playing games with huge multi-sided dice to determine the outcomes. Supposedly they've been around forever."

"The first commercially produced role-playing game on Earth was Dungeons & Dragons, back in 1974," I informed her.

"New rule," the girl proclaimed. "You have to tell me whenever you're pulling something from the copy of Wikipedia you downloaded into your memory before we left Earth. Otherwise, it's like cheating."

I had no answer to that.

"How much longer to Old Furnace?"

"About seventy-two stadia," I said, rounding down to make it sound a little closer.

"Tow?" she requested, moving closer alongside.

"Go ahead," I told her, recalling that the girl hadn't eaten lunch yet and was burning a lot of calories. eBeth reached for the metal hoop on the side of the toolbox mounted on the back of my bike and pulled it out. The internal reel and spring fed her a few yards, or, should I say, ten podes of cable, and she fit the ring over the custom post Paul had added to the steering stem on her bike. From there, a mainspring salvaged from an experimental version of a wind-up turret clock did the work of keeping the cable taut, even if she chose to do a little pedaling.

I picked up my speed to the maximum I thought I could allow myself without arousing suspicion if somebody saw us. A half an hour later we arrived at town hall. Old Furnace was the county seat, boasting approximately five thousand households within its expansive boundaries, and there were several stone buildings on the main street, including the local seat of government with its impressive clock tower. I led eBeth in a quick circuit around the building to ensure that all four faces of the clock showed the same time.

"The linkages are still attached," she observed in a professional manner, "but the south face looks a minute or two behind the others, so the collar must have slipped."

"Or the last person to fool around up there didn't have an assistant below and got tired of running up and down the stairs. What else?"

"Well, it's stopped, but that's obvious."

We parked our bikes in visitor slots and I hit the quick release on my toolbox mount and grabbed the handles. "You get the doors," I told her.

"The apprentice is supposed to carry the tools," eBeth pointed out, even though she knew as well as I that with

33

all the spare brass parts I carried, my clock-repair kit weighed half as much as she did.

Nobody paid us any attention as she searched for the door to the tower stairs, which turned out to be exactly where I would have guessed based on the building's exterior. The temperature in the tower seemed to go up a few degrees at each landing, and when we reached the small room with the turret clock, I knew it must be un-pleasantly hot for the girl.

"Why don't you go back down and eat your lunch by the river?" I suggested.

"Are you going to follow me around for the rest of my life and do my job for me?"

"At least drink some water."

eBeth scowled, but she fished a water bottle out of her pack and took several swallows. While she drank, I re-moved the wooden cover that protected the clock mechanism from bird droppings and dust. It would take a minute for her eyes to adjust to the light that filtered into the room and I considered setting up the spirit lamp packed in my tool box. Despite the fact that the hands outside weren't moving, the clock ticked away with the movement of the escapement, the pendulum describing short, sure arcs. I watched out of the corner of my eye as the girl puzzled her way through the gear train.

"There," she declared, pointing triumphantly. "The pin fell out of that gear and it's just spinning on the arbor."

"Excellent," I congratulated her. "Why did the pin fail?"

eBeth crouched down and fanned her fingers through the dust below the clock stand, then grinned. "Gotcha," she said, holding up the remains of a cotter pin. "It was a replacement and the metal fatigued where the ends were bent over. Didn't you say to ignore the whole dissimilar metals thing and use steel pins on brass and vise versa?"

"Steel on steel is terrible because there's no give and the pins fall out, unless they rust in place, and brass on brass leads to both the pin and the hole deforming," I told her, sliding open the pin selection drawer.

My apprentice locked-out the movement, sized and installed the proper pin, and then reversed her actions and gave the pendulum a couple of gentle impulses to get the clock ticking again.

"Why did they use a wood stick for the pendulum arm?" she asked.

"The length is more stable than most metals, at least in this climate, so it keeps better time."

"And what's with the stack of random washers? It looks like somebody was playing ring toss on those little posts clamped to the pendulum arm."

"Those are regulation weights, to change the center of gravity for the pendulum. More weight raises the center of gravity, shortening the period so the clock gains."

"How come I haven't seen any before?"

"Some clocks have them, some don't. This is just the first time you've noticed."

"This is your teaching method? I have to ask before you explain anything?"

"Sue suggested it," I admitted. "I'm going to give the clock a quick cleaning before I reset the time. You really should go down and eat before you get heatstroke."

"Hurry up and we'll go shopping," eBeth instructed me as she started down the stairs. "It would be too ironic if a clock engineer ran out of time to buy his wife a Ferrymen's Day present before the holiday."

"Very funny. Why don't you scope out the stores and meet me by our bikes in an hour. Then we'll go and purchase whatever you've picked out."

"Now you're thinking," my apprentice said. "How much gold did you bring?"

I didn't like the sound of that.

Four

My team members were all running late for our Tuesday night meeting and I sent Spot to fetch eBeth. I couldn't help wondering if she had forgotten to wind her watch again, and I resolved on the spot to build her an automatic movement that would wind itself. Peter had come over for dinner earlier, and then the two young Earthlings had gone on a fishing date at the creek. I was still surprised by how easily they had transitioned from fighting against ogres and skeleton bosses on the Internet to battling the local version of trout with no evidence of success, but at least once a week they headed off into the dusk with their fishing tackle.

I caught a faint flash of infrared in my peripheral vision and turned to see Sue and Stacey coming down the road from the opposite direction. They were conversing silently about something, and the only word I caught before they spotted me waiting outside and broke off communications was "Mark." In accordance with the security protocols I had put into place, my team members were keeping all artificial signaling to an absolute minimum, but low-power infrared for point-to-point communications wouldn't be spotted by any orbital monitoring systems.

"You're late," I said as they stepped up onto the wooden porch in front of The Eatery that gave customers a place to kick off the mud in the rainy season.

"Our weaving circle finished the carpet today," Sue told me, taking possession of my left arm and giving me a peck on the cheek. "We burned the midnight oil this past week getting it done, but all of the women are looking forward to the extra money it will bring in before the holiday."

"You really should have stopped by to hear the singing," Stacey said. "I'm glad I came back in time for Sue to invite me along."

"I watch the recordings," I reminded her. "I've seen it all through Sue's eyes."

"It's not the same thing as being there," my second-in-command insisted. "You have to experience life in order to appreciate it, Mark."

"I went once," I protested.

"No you didn't."

"I'm sure I remember. There was a problem with the spool rack and you surprised everybody by fixing it."

"You're confusing a memory I shared with your own experience," Sue said, giving me a smile as if she somehow approved of this technical glitch on my part.

"I've been making a collection of the authenticity videos that all of the artisans record for shipment with their products," Stacey announced. "It's so much easier than acquiring and transporting physical artifacts."

"I'm glad to hear you learned something from our stay on Earth," I applauded her. "Maybe this mission will be your last punishment assignment. But how are you accessing the Ferrymen's Eyes? If you've broken the encryption then you're risking giving away our presence."

"Why do you insist on using that ridiculous name? They're off-the-shelf 'My Life' recorders produced on Alpha Seti Seven that the Ferrymen's purchasing agents hand out like popcorn. And I didn't have to break the encryption because nobody ever changes the factory default password."

"Which is?"

"Admin," both of my team members answered at the same time, an answer I should have guessed from my three years posing as a computer repair technician on Earth.

"And the women in the weaving circle aren't uncomfortable knowing that the Ferrymen are recording every word spoken and knot tied?" I asked.

"They grew up with the recorders and they know that it means a premium price for their goods," Stacey explained. "Now that I've tracked the process from orders through the final delivery, I can say that the whole system is elegant in its simplicity. Every step in the chain is captured by 'My Life" recorders supplied by the purchasing agents. The recorders are sent to the spaceport for processing at each stage, and editors stitch the video together for shipping with the finished products before wiping the memories for reuse."

"So there are computers at the spaceport," I said. "What sort of network are they running?"

"They don't have any computers, just a giant building full of dedicated 'My Life' editing stations. It looks to me like they maintain the chain of custody from the initial order right up until shipping, and they keep adding video to the physical media that will ship with the product."

"The Ferrymen sit around editing videos?" I asked in disbelief.

"Of course not. They hire humans for the work. This is all in my report."

"Why haven't I seen it?"

"Because you banned us from making electronic transmissions," Stacey reminded me. "As much as I enjoy touring the countryside on a bicycle, I haven't been able to attend your last eleven meetings because I was at the provincial capital infiltrating the spaceport."

"Right. Wait until the others get here and then we'll all hear it at once," I said. "I don't know what's keeping Paul and Helen, but I'll go across the street to fetch the others."

"eBeth isn't back yet?" Sue asked.

"I sent Spot to get her. I wish I understood what she and her young man see in sitting on the bank of a creek and getting assaulted by alien insects while failing to catch fish they would release in any case."

"Most of the insects lose interest at the first taste of human blood, and I seriously doubt that they're fishing."

"I think you're wrong there," I told her. "I've even caught eBeth humming while she ties those flies that the fish ignore. It seems to me she's pretty passionate about the sport."

"She's pretty passionate about something," Stacey said, and I saw her elbow Sue, who seemed to be struggling to suppress a reply.

Across the road a bell jingled as the door of the apothecary shop opened and a late customer hurried off into the night clutching a small blue bottle. Justin and Kim followed a moment later, the latter pausing a moment to flip the sign in the small window from 'Open' to 'Back in Two Candles.'

The only recumbent bicycle on the planet shot down the road at breakneck speed and skidded to a halt in front of The Eatery. Paul climbed out of the teardrop cab, which he tried to pass off on everybody as lacquered papier-mâché even though I knew perfectly well it was fiberglass.

"Missed you," he greeted Stacey. "I'm going to have to start training homing pigeons if Mark continues to insist on radio silence."

"That's so sweet," she said, giving him a hug, but twisting away from a longer embrace and whispering, "Later."

"What?" I asked Sue, who looked oddly depressed by Paul and Stacey's obvious play-acting.

"We better go in," she said in a long suffering voice just as Kim and Justin reached us. "Has anybody seen Helen?"

"She stopped by the machine shop looking for eBeth earlier," Paul volunteered. "I told her that Peter and the girl were down by the creek canoodling."

"They don't have a canoe unless you built them one," I objected. "And if you did, it better not be fiberglass."

"Idiot," Sue said in exasperation. As she hauled me roughly into the dining room, I reviewed the conversation and failed to find any mistakes on my own part. I computed the probability was over eighty-seven percent that she intended 'idiot' as a term of endearment or a pet name.

"This place is unsanitary," Kim declared, running a finger across a table and then sniffing at the tip. She reached into her large shoulder satchel and brought out a bottle of homemade disinfectant, the main ingredient of which was pungent white vinegar that she fermented herself, starting with alcohol provided under protest by yours truly. The former health inspector began splashing all the tables with liberal doses of the clear liquid, and Justin followed behind her with a rag, swabbing it all around.

"I'll just go out and come in again when you're finished," Paul said, but rather than putting his words into action, he headed behind the bar and helped himself to a mug of ale. "Anybody else want one?"

"Go easy on the inebriation algorithm," I begged him. "We have milestones to discuss tonight."

"Are we getting inebriated?" Helen asked from the door as she entered. "Ugh, I hate that smell," she added, wrinkling up the nose of her encounter suit in perfect imitation of a human. "I bet our meetings would be more productive if you had fresh baked cookies to set the aroma."

"Next time," Sue promised her. "How does a batch of carob-chip sound?"

"Yummy. eBeth and Peter were right behind me, but you know how they dawdle in the dark."

"Lack of infrared vision," I excused the girl's tardiness.

"I don't think that's it," Helen replied with a smile.

"Idiot," Sue repeated, more forcefully than the previous time. The probability she was using it as a term of endearment plummeted.

"Well, if you're all done abusing your mission commander for the evening, how about—good, Spot," I interrupted myself as he herded the young couple through the door. "Feel up to guard duty?"

The dog gave me one of his patented "You'll be getting my bill in the mail," looks and headed back outside. Everybody else settled in around the two tables I'd pushed together.

"Catch anything?" I asked Peter, who for some reason turned redder than his sunburn as eBeth giggled. Sue kicked me under the table, which I took as an instruction to skip the small-talk and proceed immediately with the meeting. "Does anybody have any new business to report before we hear from Stacey?"

"I just found out that the Ferrymen's Day holiday is actually ten days, and they close the school for two weeks," eBeth said.

"A lot of the businesses we deal with in other villages and towns close for all of the first week," Paul confirmed.

"We'll be open," Justin said. "Humans tend to need a lot of medicinal herbs during the holidays."

"The Eatery will remain open as well," I decided. "Maybe a couple of you can come in and help if Frenay and her husband want to take the time off."

"Can I invite my students for a party?" eBeth asked. "All of the other teachers do it."

"As long as it's not during the evening rush," I told her. "This place isn't exactly making me a ton of money."

"It's not too late to move to the provincial capital," Stacey said. "There's no shortage of gold flowing through the spaceport, and you could easily find work as an engineer. All of you would earn ten times what you're making in this backwater."

"And we'd be a hundred times more likely to be spotted as alien AI. If nobody else has anything to add, why don't you bring us up to date on how you spent the last three months?"

"Well, I've been collecting," Stacey said, which came as a surprise to nobody. "I started out by looking for key cultural artifacts because that's what I'm into, but I ended up focusing on raw footage from the 'My Life' recorders that the Ferrymen purchasing agents hand out to everybody involved in producing goods for off-planet exports."

"The AI who needed six tractor-trailer loads to ship home her loot from Earth gave up just like that?" Justin asked skeptically.

"It took a long while to sink in but these people really are different," Stacey replied earnestly. "They don't place any special value on being first in art, if that makes sense. They honor the creator's imagination and skills, and almost every development in their cultural history has a name attached to it, but in terms of the work itself, they assume that every copy will be better than its predecessor."

"But what about the works by masters?" eBeth interjected. "On Earth, the museums were full of paintings and sculptures that were worth more than dozens of people could hope to earn in a lifetime."

"Doesn't happen here," Stacey said. "They have no word for counterfeiting, and creative people, from musicians to mechanics, believe that there's no greater praise than having your work copied."

"That explains why nobody could tell me where to apply for patents." Paul took a long swallow from his ale and shook his head ruefully. "I thought they were playing games with me so I did some playing back. I guess I have a few apologies to make."

"Let me tell you about the art museum in the capital," Stacey continued. "Every painting, carving, statue, and piece of pottery on display is numbered. I asked about it at the main desk and they explained that the number is for the corresponding work in the gift shop catalog. I've never been one to collect copies but I went there because I was curious to see how good the replicas were. The gift shop turned out to be a warehouse attached to the museum, and while I was looking around, employees kept on coming in with slips and taking pieces out of numbered racks. I finally asked why the patrons didn't come to pick up their own purchases, and a clerk explained to me that museum visitors just take the exhibit off the wall and pay on the way out. The cashier makes a note and sends to the gift shop for a replacement."

"You mean that they continually restock the museum with new copies?" Helen asked. "That's different."

"But what about the original?" eBeth protested.

"If it was ever in the museum, it would have been sold a long time ago, but my guess is that pieces have to be copied quite a few times before they attain the status to be included in museum collections," Stacey explained. "Of course, some of the copies are quite expensive if the work is technically difficult to replicate, but nobody worries about which was the first and it creates a lot of well-paid work for artisans."

"Did you find any more signs of imported goods from the rest of the galaxy in the capital?" I asked her.

"Yes, but without an electrical grid or a network infra-structure, there's pretty limited demand for alien goods." She glanced over at Paul, as if seeking support before going out on a limb, and he nodded. "And I have a theory about it."

"Why the Ferrymen aren't importing goods that would work here, including magically enhanced objects?"

"I didn't see any crystal balls labeled, 'Made in Eniniac,' in the shops, but that's not what I'm talking about."

There was a rumbling growl and I looked over to see that Spot had his head in the front door.

"You're supposed to be patrolling the perimeter, and she said 'made,' not 'mage,'" I scolded him. The dog withdrew. "I wish I'd never told Spot that he's a dead ringer for the Archmage of Eniniac. I think it's gone to his head."

"I've found that when I'm teaching it pays to stay on topic," eBeth volunteered brightly.

"Sorry," I muttered. "Please continue, Stacey."

"While there aren't any high-tech goods on offer, I've seen signs of alien influence all over. For example, there's a store that sells beautiful locally-made wood furniture that I would swear is copied from Hanker designs."

"Hankers like Pffift?" eBeth asked. "When he visited Mark's apartment on Earth, we had to put two normal chairs side by side for him to sit, and he didn't look very comfortable."

"The proportions are different, and the chair-backs are altered to accommodate human spines, but the aesthetic remains pure Hanker. Then there was the gift shop that was selling silver chopsticks with ornate serving bowls as a set."

"Pharide?" Sue asked.

Stacey nodded. "They were made by a local silversmith, but the chopsticks had those little indents on the ends that the Pharides designed for serving individual fish eggs, and the bowls all come with an attached saucer for holding ice chips."

"Maybe the locals are copying ideas from the export goods they're producing for the Ferrymen," I suggested.

"Pffift would have known if the Ferrymen were exporting Hanker furniture," Paul pointed out. "And the Pharides are allergic to silver. I've always wondered if human myths about werewolves are based on Pharides sneaking onto Earth at some point. They look the part."

"Maybe the Ferrymen are making goods for humans on one of the other two reservation worlds we know about and selling them here to keep trade in balance," Peter suggested. "My eleventh grade economics teacher told us that export-based economies all run into serious problems."

"That's an interesting idea," I said, impressed that he remembered anything from high school. "Although I suspect your teacher believed that because your own country is dependent on imports. If we were talking about any species other than the Ferrymen, it would be worth investigating."

"What's so special about the Ferrymen?" eBeth demanded in support of her boyfriend.

"They're lazy," Helen told her. "I mean, compared to them, I'm a workaholic."

"And they don't like change," Justin added. "They're more set in their ways than old humans. That's how they ended up with the name."

"Ferrymen?" eBeth asked.

"Exactly," I told her. "Most species have names that translate to something like 'human' in their native tongue, but the Ferrymen have been playing the same game for so long that it's become their name."

"They coast around the galaxy cataloging planets and waiting for life to develop to the point that it would be useful in creating saleable goods of one sort or another," Helen elaborated. "Then they watch for growing pains, step in as Sky Gods, and transplant breeding populations and enough of the local ecosystem to make a new start on a compatible world. The only real value they add is preventing wars until the client species forgets how to fight them."

"That doesn't sound lazy at all," eBeth objected.

"It plays out very slowly and they get the species they're transporting to do all of the heavy lifting," I told her. "The Ferrymen spend most of their lives lazing around in starships and watching reruns of holographic entertainment produced by other cultures. The only part of their approach that varies is the goods produced by their latest clients."

"Then where are the people in the provincial capital getting the alien design ideas?"

"I think they're traveling," Stacey dropped her bombshell. "It wouldn't be unheard of for the Ferrymen to take workers from their client population along as back office support to help manage inventory and sales. They really are that lazy."

"Library would have noticed if humans had been popping up all over the galaxy the last couple thousand years," I pointed out. "It took them less than three years to nail me for the contract workers I was sending off-Earth during the quiet period."

"What if they were disguised?" Peter asked.

"The portal filters would have caught—unless they aren't using the portals," I interrupted myself. "Have you seen humans boarding Ferrymen ships at the spaceport?"

Stacey nodded. "I was tempted to pick a ship at random and watch it from the moment it landed to the moment it lifted off, but they're on the surface for days at a time loading cargo, and you ordered us not to take any risks that could lead to being spotted."

"New mission parameters," I announced. "We've gathered enough information through passive observation and we can always substitute in data from our final report on Earth for biological characteristics of humans and their domestic animals. It's time to focus on the Ferrymen."

"These humans here are much healthier than Earthlings," Kim objected. "I'm still analyzing the data."

"I meant we can cut-and-paste their basic genetics and natural history, which was identical up until just a couple thousand years ago," I corrected myself. "And you keep studying the Originals, Helen, but make sure the locals don't catch you at it. Stacey, I want you back at the provincial capital, and I'm authorizing you, all of you, to start asking questions." A thought suddenly occurred to me and I added, "How many Ferrymen are in residence around the spaceport?"

"That's the other thing," Stacey said. "I haven't seen any yet, though it's not that surprising since I'm trying to keep a low profile myself."

"We need numbers for how many Ferrymen are on this world. It's not credible that they're acting entirely through agents and never leaving their cargo ships."

"I hadn't realized how spoiled we were by access to the Internet and all the badly protected databases on Earth," Helen said wistfully. "The only way to learn anything here is to see it happen with your own eyes."

"How about me?" eBeth asked.

"You keep teaching, and Peter can take care of the machine shop. Paul, as soon as the holiday is over I want you to go to the capital with Stacey and report back in person as soon as you have answers. I'm going to work with Helen to see if we can get a better grip on the Originals, but everybody should keep an eye out for imported goods or alien ideas that don't fit in. Just try not to make anybody suspicious that you're staging an interrogation."

"I still have the feeling that the villagers are hiding something from me," Sue said.

"I think you've done an excellent job winning the trust of the local women," I told her. "This world has been experimenting with different types of photography for hundreds of years, so maybe you can pretend that you're interested in family albums and dig for details that way."

"I am interested in family albums. I've started one for us."

I blinked a few times while processing the implications of Sue's last comment and decided to pretend that I hadn't heard. "Justin and Kim will continue working in their apothecary clinic and they can finish filling out the standard reports for the rest of us."

Justin groaned, but Kim looked pleased since it meant more time to experiment with miracle cures.

"I know that it's frustrating trying to learn about a place without an information infrastructure we can hack into, but this is why they pay us the big bucks," I concluded.

"Did we get a raise?" Paul asked.

"It's just an expression."

Five

"...and our faaaaaarrrrrrr away home." I warbled, extending both arms as I reached for the note at the end of the ballad.

The Eatery's patrons burst into applause, and I could see from their faces that it was genuine enjoyment and not the minimal amount of alcohol they had consumed. I never used to think of myself as a singer, but running a bar without televisions and music was a challenge. I'd put an effort into learning the local songs to fill the entertainment vacuum on slow nights and it was paying holiday dividends.

"Encore," Hosea shouted, pounding the bar with one hand and pushing his mug forward with the other. He'd accounted for a third of the dozen ales I'd sold all evening.

"That was an encore, the fourth one," Xeres said, bodily lifting his friend to his feet. "It's Ferrymen's Eve and I'm sure that Mark wants to spend time with his family."

"You should sing at the festival tomorrow," Palti told me, her eyes shining from emotion. "Make him sing, Sue."

"I'll try, but he can be really shy when he's not behind the bar," my second-in-command said. "We're all really looking forward to the festival after spending so many years in the north."

"Don't they celebrate Ferrymen's Day?" Sophus asked.

"Of course, but we were always outsiders, being from the southern continent," I lied smoothly. "I hope I didn't get too emotional while singing but it's good to be home."

The rest of the villagers and local farmers insisted on exchanging handshakes or hugs as they took their leave, and Sue seemed so reluctant to let them go that I worried for a moment she was going to ask them all to stay the night.

"You did good, Mark," eBeth complimented me once the place was emptied out. "If I didn't know you, I'd think you'd been leading community sing-alongs since you were a child."

"We have something similar on Library, though it involves taking turns applying numerical methods to solve confluent hypergeometric—"

"That's my cue," eBeth spoke over me and headed for the stairs. "Goodnight, Sue. Are you coming, Spot?"

The dog rose from his favorite spot on the oversized stone hearth, shook himself out, then followed the girl upstairs.

"I have something special for you," Sue informed me, a twinkle in her artificial eyes.

I swear that the linear processor which handled motion control for my encounter suit skipped a clock cycle as I wondered what new lesson she had in store for me. Sue disappeared into the small room we used as an office for managing the business and reappeared a minute later looking exactly the same. I didn't know whether to be disappointed or relieved.

"It came this afternoon while you were out," she said, handing me a new copy of the Engineer's Journal. "They approved your subscription to the Clockmaker's and Watchmaker's Guild edition."

"Are you sure?" I asked, holding the magazine cover closer in the flickering light. There, under the main title, was the guild category designation, bringing to six the number of different magazines I'd been approved to receive. Anybody could subscribe to the basic Engineer's Journal, but you had to complete a correspondence test to demonstrate journeyman knowledge in your specialty before they would deliver any of the limited editions. I believe it had less to do with guild protectionism than with rationing, as the magazines were printed without the benefit of high-speed offset presses.

"You told me clockmakers and watchmakers barely talk to each other and that you hadn't met anybody other than yourself who does both," Sue said, smiling as I flipped through the pages like an eager boy. "Why would they share a magazine?"

"Clockmakers build gear trains that do work, like ringing bells and running automatons," I explained. "Watchmakers mainly care about telling the time with as small a mechanism as possible. But the Engineering Journal only has so many publications, and watchmakers and clockmakers have more in common with each other than they do with mill engineers or ship builders."

"And you subscribe to both of those as well," Sue pointed out. "Why did you wait so long to take the test for the specialty you do the most work in?"

"I thought that taking more than a test a month might look suspicious," I told her. "Besides, I'm making a survey of this planet's technology and I already see clocks every day. This is great timing because the village council wants me to buy an old turret clock that I can restore for the steeple of the Ferrymen Temple. This magazine will have the best classified ads for our purposes."

"Why didn't you mention the clock job before?"

"I'm still having trouble adjusting to verbally recounting everything that goes on each day," I admitted. "I don't know how you and eBeth adapted so quickly. If it turns out that the Ferrymen have let their guard down, I'll be the happiest AI on the planet when I lift the ban on radio frequency communications."

"You know, you could just share your memory with me," Sue suggested, causing the old processor to skip another clock cycle. "It's not unheard of when two AI feel about each other the way we do."

"I think it's prohibited on duty," I said, my voice coming out funny due to the unexpected lump in the throat of my encounter suit.

"It's not like you're famous throughout the galaxy for following the rules," my second-in-command practically purred. Then she broke the mood by turning away and starting to put the chairs up on the tables, leading me to conclude that she'd been teasing all along. "You enjoy your journal and I'll straighten up. I've noticed that humans value anticipation as much as actual accomplishments and I'm starting to understand why."

I moved behind the bar with my magazine and parked myself in front of the candelabra. While I wasn't entirely sure what Sue was talking about, I've noted that since coming to this world, I've developed a marked preference for reading my journals word-for-word, rather than simply scanning each page and running a text recognition process. Before I knew it, the last candle was guttering out and the room was empty. I decided to light the rarely used oil lantern above the bar, which was both more expensive than candles and lacked the atmospherics. Then I eagerly returned to the article about the use of lock-out levers versus slipping mainsprings in self-winding watches.

The front door creaked open and I heard somebody enter with a cat-like tread. "We're closed," I called out, trying to keep the annoyance from my voice. There was no response, but something made me look up and I saw that an Original had entered The Eatery. For a moment I was actually speechless.

Originals have been described as a cross between a very hairy man and a three-toed sloth, though I think the comparison is unfair to the arboreal mammals. Despite being equipped with a large claw on each of their three fingers, Originals walk upright and are capable of moving with surprising quickness. That speed brought my nocturnal visitor all the way to the bar before I could decide what to say.

"What can I get you?" I asked. One of the few imaging tools at my disposal in the absence of active scanning was to examine the creature in the infrared spectrum, effectively seeing through its hair. His hair. The Original was a male.

He pulled one of my bill-tabulating slates off the pile, picked up a piece of chalk, and began to draw something. Fortunately, his claws were so curved that the chalk actually protruded between them without their scraping against the slate and waking eBeth.

"Ale?" I read.

The hairy creature nodded.

"In English? You wrote 'Ale' in English rather than drawing a tankard or a keg?" I demanded incredulously.

This time my infrared vision detected a look of impatience under all that hair. It was the last thing one would expect from a sloth of any type, so I put aside my magazine and drew my visitor a lukewarm one.

"That'll be four coppers," I said, presenting the tankard.

The Original made an unmistakable, "Put it on my tab," gesture at the slate, lifted the tankard, and drained half of the contents in one go. Then we spent a couple minutes regarding each other in uncomfortable silence. Finally my visitor downed the remaining half and let out a satisfied belch.

"Not much of a talker, are you?" I inquired.

A quick rub with the side of a hairy hand left the slate cleaner than it had been since the last time it was washed. "No," my visitor scrawled. "Again."

I refilled the tankard, weighing the odds as to whether the surprise guest would be more responsive to questioning after a few drinks or if I'd end up with a passed-out Original and the county safety inspector knocking on my door. I'd never heard of one of the natives intentionally making contact with humans, much less walking into a business and demanding service, so it must have sought me out on Ferrymen's Eve for more than a drink.

"Do you have a name I can call you?"

The native hesitated a moment, and then wrote, "Art."

"And do you want to tell me why you're here?"

The Original suddenly stiffened and then slid off the tall barstool as if he was about to flee. My response was delayed as I tried to sort out the conflicting demands of my mission, the Ferrymen's ban on interactions with the natives, and the League's first contact protocols, but then I saw that he hadn't been reacting to my question at all. Spot had come downstairs with a tennis ball in his mouth, and something about the dog must have awakened a primal fear in the Original.

"It's okay, Art," I attempted to calm my guest. "That's just Spot. I know he's a different breed than any of the dogs you've seen around here, but I, uh, we brought him back from the northern continent."

The Original dipped his body slightly in the dog's direction, almost as if he was bowing, and then climbed back onto the stool. Spot rolled his ball in our direction and then surprised me by heading back upstairs. Art and I both watched the course of the tennis ball as it bounced off the legs of three different tables before deflecting off the wall and ending up behind the bar where it came to rest at my feet.

"Bouncy," Art wrote on the slate, and I could almost hear a sardonic inquiry in the scratching of the chalk.

"It's a chew-toy," I explained. "We brought it from the north. Some of the fish in colder waters use air bladders for buoyancy. The people up there have a gluing technique to cover the bladder with fibers so the sled dogs don't puncture the skin while they gnaw."

The Original took a pull at his ale, gave me a hairy look that I interpreted as skepticism, and printed, "Whatever."

"Is it alright if I ask a few questions about you and your kind? How is it that in the thousands of years humans have lived on this planet, nobody realized that you understand speech?"

Art shrugged and took another sip from his tankard.

"But my family and I speak a rare dialect from the north, and even there, almost nobody knows the written form," I persisted. "Not only do you understand what I'm saying, you can print as well as the best student in eBeth's class."

The Original tapped a single claw on the bar in exact time with the ticking of the grandfather clock in the corner.

Something about Art's body language gave me the impression that he was offering commentary about the speed of my thought process, implying that I was a bit dull-witted. Then the solution hit me and I had to wonder if Art's assessment was accurate.

"You learned English in eBeth's class? You could hardly go unnoticed. The windows let in plenty of light, but even I'd have trouble trying to read through that thick glass."

"Even I?" Art printed, adding the dot below the question mark like a gunshot. I was beginning to feel outclassed in the interrogation department.

"I come from a family with excellent vision." Then I had a second epiphany. "You hide in the garden in the back of the auditorium during classes."

The Original set down his tankard and offered me a three-clap round of applause.

"Look," I said, tiring of the game. "The Ferrymen have rules—you know who the Ferrymen are?"

Below all that facial hair Art's features rearranged themselves in an expression that I easily read as, "Oh, please."

"The Ferrymen have rules about interfering with your people but those obviously don't apply when you come into my place and order a drink. You may not have a lot of experience in bars, but it's normal for the bartender to ask a few questions to make the patron feel welcome."

Art let one of his forearms fall toward the bar with the palm up, as if to say, "Ask away," or maybe he was suggesting that I pay for the privilege of interrogating him? I decided to go with the former interpretation and move to the latter only if it proved necessary.

"Are all of your people mute?"

The Original opened his mouth and produced a noise that was vaguely reminiscent of the ancient dial-up modems I had encountered on Earth when servicing fax machines. I felt a slight tickle in the radio frequency spectrum at the same time, but either it didn't contain any information or the signal-to-noise level was too low. The overall effect was like nothing I'd ever experienced or heard of.

"Telepathic?" I guessed.

Art pursed his lips in an odd manner and tilted his head slightly to the left and right, like a human expressing the concept of so-so.

"Are you in communication with the Ferrymen?"

He picked up the slate again, rubbed it clean, and then took a moment, apparently rethinking what he'd intended to write. Finally Art scratched out, "No," and took another sip of his ale.

"How about with other humans?"

Again he took his time before printing his own question in response. "Like you?"

I hesitated myself, unsure whether or not Art had somehow sensed that I wasn't a member of the same species as the refugees from Earth. It seemed unlikely that he could have seen through my encounter suit, but then again, maybe that odd sound he had made earlier was some sort of natural scan, like a bat's sonar.

"Yes," I said, and then hedged since I was more interested in getting the correct answer than semantics. "There's more variation in humans than in your own people. We come in all shapes and sizes, while the small number of your species I've seen all look pretty much alike."

This seemed to tickle the Original, and he printed, "We get that a lot."

"From who?" I asked, before it occurred to me that he was making a joke. "Okay. You ever hear the one about the rabbi, the priest and the imam?"

The slate was erased again, and this time, Art laboriously printed, "Is this an ethnic joke?"

"No, I don't tell those. It's a religion joke, well, really it's more about the grocery business, but—" I stopped talking to look at the new message he printed.

"Salt?" I read out loud. "But that's the punch line! How could you know about kosher and halal meat processing?"

The Original shook his shaggy head in irritation and drummed his claws on the bar before taking the chalk up again and writing, "For me. Snack."

"Oh, sorry," I said, feeling guilty about falling down on the job and retrieving my bar munchies from the high shelf that kept Spot from temptation. "I've got these little dried fish, salt-brined hard-boiled eggs, and baked dough twists."

Art picked up the basket with the fish, sniffed, and then put it down and pushed it as far away as he could reach with his disproportionately long arms. Then he studied the jar of eggs, dipping one claw in the brine and licking it off before giving a ho-hum shrug. Finally he took up one of Sue's homemade pretzels and examined it closely. He picked at one of the large salt crystals with the tip of a claw before taking a cautious nibble. Then a look of shock passed over his hairy features and he pointed behind me.

Cursing myself once again for the self-imposed radio frequency silence that prevented me from using my active sensing suite, I spun around to investigate the threat. I was still trying to figure out what had frightened the Original when I heard the door again and realized that I'd been tricked. The tankard was empty and the basket of pretzels was gone. For a moment I considered going after Art, but then I saw the silver coin on the bar, which amounted to an eight-hundred-percent tip.

Rerunning the conversation in my head, I confirmed that by Library standards I was well within bounds for a first contact and the whole exchange wouldn't raise an eyebrow if it came up for review. I wasn't too concerned about Ferrymen laws since the secret presence of my team on Reservation was already a violation of their local sovereignty. Besides, I was confident that Art would be back in contact when he had something to say, probably after consultation with others of his kind. If I needed to talk to him beforehand, at least I knew where he hung out during eBeth's classes.

Six

The Ferrymen landing ships flew low over the village common in tight formation and then broke apart in a dozen crazy directions, some colliding with each other as they went out of control. Children pointed and laughed as their parents struggled to control the giant kites which were painted to look like spacecraft, but dependent on the wind and string tension to stay aloft.

Sue and I observed the festivities from a blanket she'd spread on the grass which had been grazed to stubble by a wrecking crew of cows and goats. The parade of kites devolved into a contest for survival as the ground crews battled by sawing at each other's strings, and before long the sole survivor, with a hole poked in its paper airfoil, came in for a victorious crash landing.

"It's a good thing your cousin's apprentice waited to launch because I would have disqualified him from the competition," the headmaster informed us, taking a seat on the grass nearby without the benefit of a blanket. "That thing is a monster."

"Doesn't anybody fly box kites around here?" I asked.

"But it's got ten times the sail surface of the other kites. It's lifting eBeth completely off the ground!"

I started to my feet, prepared to break radio silence if I had to call for help, but I immediately saw that Joshua had been exaggerating. The kite probably had enough lift to make off with the girl if she'd been the only one holding the braided cord, but eBeth and Peter had roped themselves together to prevent any such accident. As the kite gained altitude, I noticed that it was demonstrating more maneuverability than the single line could account for, and it occurred to me that Paul was nowhere in sight. I wasn't picking up any radio frequency signals, but I did detect a suspicious red dot flickering over the control surfaces of the kite that practically shouted "ruby laser."

"Our daughter tells me that you've been attending her class," Sue was saying to the headmaster when I sat down again. "Are you planning a trip north?"

"Studying a new language keeps my brain pointy," he replied in English. "We were fortunate to rent her."

"Hire," Sue corrected him. "You can rent a house or a bicycle, but you hire a person. And we want our brains to stay sharp, not pointy."

Joshua pulled a small notebook out of his pocket and penciled in these gems of wisdom. "Thank you. Your husband never corrects my errors. Isn't that right, Mark?"

"I learned Northern as an adult so I'm not confident about the fine differences," I said, which was at least half true. "Sue's the one with a gift for languages."

This compliment got a blush out of my second-in-command's encounter suit, or perhaps she was embarrassed by my lying about her being the team's linguistic expert. For some reason, the redness in her cheeks triggered a reaction in my visual processing center which fed back into a heightened feeling of protectiveness towards her on the part of my threat-assessment subsystem. This led me to check the last time I'd run a self-diagnostic on the suit, and I almost fell over when I realized I'd been putting it off day-by-day since before we left Earth.

"Actually, I had an ulterior motive in plopping myself down next to your blanket," Joshua said. "It being Ferrymen's Day and all, I naturally got to thinking about our clock project. I wanted to ask if you'd had a chance to do any shopping."

"I think I found what we're looking for last night," I told him. "I sent Spot to the local post office with a letter and a deposit this morning, but he came home in a foul mood with the messenger bag untouched, so I assume the branch was closed."

"Yes, everything shuts down for Ferrymen's Day. Wasn't it the same when you were growing up?"

I mumbled something about my parents being nonconformists.

"So tell me about our clock," the headmaster continued, though I had the feeling that he'd be making a note of my latest slip in his little book.

"Well, there's always a chance somebody else will snap it up, and this was my first issue of the Clockmaker's and Watchmaker's Guild edition, so it's possible the ad ran last month as well and a sale is already in progress."

"I'm familiar with the delays involved in buying through mail-order," Joshua said dryly, a reminder that most of the school's supplies were sourced from distant distributors. "What about the clock itself?"

"A four-hundred year old Zeno," I told him, unable to suppress my pleasure at the find. "It was discovered in a barn in Province Three after an estate sale. The seller doesn't know anything about the clock's history, but from the description of the condition, I'll bet somebody bought it years ago with the intention of restoration but never got started."

"And the price?" the headmaster prompted me.

"Seven gold delivered. That leaves sixty silver for parts."

"When would it arrive?"

"In the letter I asked for it to be sent by canal because there are only a half a dozen locks between the shipper's address and the warehouse at Fisher's Point," I said, naming the nearest branch-canal terminus. "I think we could have it here within a few weeks."

Joshua's face fell. "We were hoping for sooner than that," he confessed.

"I expect the restoration process to take at least that long. eBeth will be doing all of the work as her apprentice-ship graduation project."

"Well, I can't complain about anything that involves our star teacher," the headmaster said, standing up and brushing off his pants. "I better let the others know about the schedule so they don't all come around pestering you."

"I have a question of my own, if you don't mind my asking. It's about the gardens you plant at the back of the large indoor spaces. Do they have a purpose beyond air purification and the obvious aesthetic benefit?"

"Air purification?" Joshua chuckled. "We aren't in the habit of introducing dangerous gasses to our rooms and none of our buildings are hermetically sealed. Is that something they do in the north?"

"It's colder there and they use a lot of insulation, so air flow can be an issue," I replied, realizing that I'd misread the purpose of the gardens, and hoping he wouldn't call me out on such an obvious blunder for somebody who supposedly grew up on the planet. "I guess there's a lot of variation between provinces."

"If you say so, Mark, but the reason we include gardens in public meeting places around here is to give the

Originals a place to come and observe. I'm not aware of any specific instances of their taking us up on the invitation, but if they came and went at night, nobody would be the wiser. It's a traditional gesture of goodwill that's been passed down by our ancestors."

"Did the tradition originate with the Ferrymen?" Sue followed up, her recently developed intuition telling her that I was too embarrassed to do so myself.

"I don't believe so, though it's hardly my area of scholarship," Joshua replied. "My true expertise is in pies."

"Pies?"

"Lemon meringue, apple, blueberry. Nothing out of the ordinary."

A man on the other side of the village common shouted something that was lost in the breeze, but other people between us took up the cry, and after a very few seconds, the message reached us.

"Judges to the pie contest. Judges to the pie contest."

"That's me," the headmaster said. "Happy Ferrymen's Day if we don't bump into each other again before sunset."

"Happy Ferrymen's Day," Sue and I chorused, though I caught my second-in-command multiplexing her speech to blend the words "Helen's pecan pie," into the traditional salutation. I waited until Joshua was out of earshot before reprimanding her.

"Planting subliminal suggestions in a non-emergency situation is a violation of our basic Observer ethos."

"Really, Mark. It's just a friendly contest and Helen spent all night baking that pie. Besides, don't you think we have something more important to talk about?"

"You're right." I gently took her face in my hands to disguise a shift into secure infrared communications and transmitted a complete transcript of my conversation with

Art which had taken place the previous night. She didn't react at all to the news and it took me a second to register that her eyes were closed. "Sue?"

"Aren't you going to kiss me?" she asked, opening one eye halfway.

"I was sending you an infrared data dump," I admitted, feeling a bit foolish.

Both of Sue's eyes came open and she removed my hands from her face more forcefully than necessary to accomplish her purpose. "The last time I checked we don't have to be touching for that," she said, sounding more than a little annoyed. "What's so important?"

I looked directly into her eyes and repeated the transmission, and I could sense her setting aside whatever had been on her mind in order to digest the new data.

"Put it together with what the headmaster just told us about their indoor gardens and it's probable that the Originals know a lot more about what's going on here than we do," I added in a final burst of infrared.

"Have you shared this with any of the others yet?" she asked out loud.

"No," I replied, which seemed to please her. The truth was that I hadn't run into any other members of the team since Art's visit, but I had an intuition of my own about what she wanted to hear and gambled on a minor embellishment. "I wanted to tell you first."

"It may be time to visit Library for consultation," my second-in-command sent via infrared. "The Originals are obviously a sentient species that could qualify for League membership, and without their express permission, the Ferrymen never should have brought a colonizing population to this world."

"I've been thinking about that and I want to clear up a few points the next time I speak to Art," I replied the same way. "It's possible that the Ferrymen did get permission from the Originals to settle this world with humans. That would mean that the laws and traditions regulating how the two communities interact were a matter of negotiation rather than a charitable gesture on the Ferrymen's part. Given the ability of the Originals to comprehend spoken language, and the indoor gardens that give them a convenient hiding spot to listen in on human activities, we have to assume that they are at least as cognizant about the greater galaxy as the locals."

"Hey, what are you two love birds chatting about?" Kim asked, sitting herself down on the blanket. Justin took the spot next to her, so that there were now four AI in human encounter suits and one large dog sharing a blanket. I hadn't even noticed that Spot had joined us, and he seemed to be paying pretty close attention considering that none of us were eating. When I looked in his direction, he began vigorously scratching behind his ear with one of his hind paws.

"Mark was just telling me how much he missed seeing the two of you at our party last night," Sue said, simultaneously squirting them with an infrared transmission that recapped our conversation.

"We could hear the singing from across the road, not that I'm complaining," Justin responded, overlaying an encrypted data package of his own. "You have a fine tenor, Mark."

I decrypted my team member's transmission and blurted out in English, "Are you sure?"

"It seems that I'm not the only apothecary on the planet dishing out miracle cures," Kim said with a light laugh.

Justin's data described a patient who had visited their shop the previous evening with a headache that had persisted for several days. The woman's breath had triggered a red flag in Kim's internal spectrum analyzer and she recognized the molecules as the decay product of self-terminating nanobots that had depleted their internal power sources and were exiting the body through exhalation.

"So your patient was initially treated far away," Sue said out loud, by which she was clearly implying off-world.

"Oddly enough, no," Kim replied. "The medicine had been administered in the last week. The headaches the patient was experiencing were actually a good sign as her brain adjusted to the shrinking of the tumor."

"Then the herbal remedy was imported," I said as a couple of villagers walked past our blanket.

"It certainly wasn't made up locally," Justin said, then shifted back to infrared. "But was it brought in by the Ferrymen, by a human, or some third party? Without a detection grid we're flying blind here. What if the League Council leaked our mission like they did when we were on Earth? There could be aliens coming and going all the time."

"The council doesn't know about our mission yet, unless our representative has told them. And Library's portal engineers would never connect a world without authorization. Even though we've maintained radio silence, I'm listening all the time and I wouldn't have missed the chatter from an incoming ship."

"Unless they're maintaining radio silence as well," Kim pointed out silently. "Maybe this whole world is crawling with advanced species communicating with line-of-sight signaling."

"But the Ferrymen would have noticed by now," I objected.

"Unless they aren't even here," Sue pointed out.

"We'll find out when Paul and Stacey report back from the provincial capital."

"They haven't even left yet," Justin reminded me. "In fact, here they come now."

Not knowing the locations of my team members at all times was really starting to get on my nerves, and I looked over just in time to see Paul spreading his jacket on the grass. Then he sat down cross-legged next to it while Stacey settled gracefully on the sacrificial garment. For a moment I felt like he was showing me up in front of Sue, but then I remembered that we were sitting on a blanket.

"What's that in the rucksack, Paul?" I inquired.

"Kite string," he replied, lying bare-faced about the portable laser guidance system he'd obviously smuggled in from off-world. Stacey gave him an admiring look and giggled.

I made a mental note for the next time I was on Library to check whether long periods of radio frequency silence led to insubordination from team members, not that Paul had ever been one for following instructions.

"Try to pay attention for just two seconds," I said, though it sounded whiny to my own ears, and then I flashed them both an update via infrared.

"Somebody should find Helen," Stacey suggested. "Paul and I are planning on riding out when the sun sets, so we won't be available for a meeting later."

"How about fetching Helen?" I asked Spot, who responded with a yawn. "I'll cook your favorite dinner."

This got the dog up and he trotted off in a straight line towards the woods that lined the stream. Too late I saw that Helen was barely fifty yards from us, meaning I had promised to make barbecued ribs in return for the dog taking a short jog. To add insult to injury, he stopped and relieved himself along the way.

Two minutes later, Spot led Helen back to the blanket where she sat on her heels and began rubbing his belly. Then she surprised us all by saying, "I spotted an Original at dawn heading in the direction of the river so I've kept an eye on him. He's been watching you guys all morning."

"The Originals are watching us?" I asked, feeling strangely indignant about being on the receiving end for a change.

"This one is. Anyway, I was in the line of sight for your last data dump. Even though it was pretty noisy by the time it got to me I'm pretty sure I received all of the important facts. This is a mess."

"And it's not even our fault," Paul added unnecessarily.

"Shouldn't eBeth and Peter be here?" Sue asked.

"We're conspicuous enough as it is," I said, and every direction I turned I saw curious villagers looking away to avoid eye contact. "Alright. No changes to what we decided the other night, but everybody be careful."

There was another sound of indistinct shouting that even on full gain my hearing couldn't decipher, but the human repeater system worked as it had previously, and twenty seconds later somebody just a few blankets over cried, "Helen's pecan pie."

"I won," Helen yelled, leaning over and giving the startled dog a hug. "I haven't won anything other than a bicycle race since we left Earth."

"We'll walk over with you," Stacey offered, standing up and brushing off Paul's jacket, which she then slipped into. "We both like pie."

"What's going on with everybody?" I demanded of my second-in-command. "It's like the whole team is emulating eBeth and Peter."

"We're not that bad," Sue said, and turned to Kim. "Don't you and Justin want to get in some quality time by yourselves?"

"Right," Kim said, and before I could point out that I hadn't dismissed the meeting, she pulled Justin to his feet and the two sauntered off in the direction of the games. I suspected that our public health expert intended to slip a disinfectant into the apple bobbing basin.

"I know that we aren't going to resolve anything without more data, but everybody seems to be taking my news pretty lightly," I complained to Sue. "I'm beginning to think that I'm missing something here."

"Or forgetting something." She gave me a look I couldn't quite categorize.

Sue waited patiently as I racked my short-term memory for anything I might have missed in the conversation, and then I began casting further back, looking for connections to Ferrymen's Day. Idiot!

"This is for you," I said, fumbling in my pocket for her present. "I know they must have bigger ones in the provincial capital, but—"

"Oh, Mark," she cried, and threw herself into my arms. With her face buried in my neck, I could feel the artificial tears flowing down her cheeks. "I've waited so long for this. Tell me it means what I think it does."

"Yes?" I ventured, figuring that my chances of getting it right were much better than fifty-fifty since her question implied that she desired a positive response. I wanted to ask her why she'd never bought a diamond ring herself if she wanted one so much, but I figured I had better wait until she stopped crying. Then the significance of my gift came crashing down, and I swore that I'd get even with eBeth for dragging me into that jewelry store to buy what Sue had obviously taken as an engagement ring.

Seven

"Your dog is weird," eBeth's star pupil complained after spending five minutes lying on the floor locked in a stare-down with Spot. "It's like he's laughing at us."

"Maybe it's just you, Naomi," a boy from the class suggested. "I'll bet I can make him look away."

The children changed places, but Monos didn't last two minutes. Spot let out a long sigh as if to express how little impressed he was with their efforts.

"Is this really what you guys do for fun?" eBeth asked her students in English. "Who wants to play a game?"

"We *are* playing a game," another girl insisted as she took the boy's place in front of the phlegmatic dog. "Doesn't he ever blink?"

"That's an interesting question," I said, coming around the bar with a pitcher of lemonade into which Sue must have dumped every last granule of sugar we had in The Eatery that hadn't already gone into cookie and pastry dough. "There are those who say a dog that doesn't blink is actually a wolf in disguise."

"He's making it up," eBeth reassured her startled students. "We're not telling ghost stories, Mark. Besides, it's only lunch time."

"You call your father by his first name?" Monos asked in astonishment.

"That's because I'm grown up and I'm mad at him. Naomi, please bring me one of those slates."

"Are you going to charge us for the lemonade?" a boy asked, pushing away his cup. "I don't want any now."

"The slate is for a game. It's called Hangman."

"What's a hangman?"

"A guy who—" eBeth caught herself just in time and improvised on the fly, "—it's another word for a puppeteer."

"Oh, because the puppet hangs from strings," the student surmised. "Are you going to put on a puppet show?"

"I'm going to draw a puppet, but I can only do one string or it will get too confusing," eBeth told them, and drew a single vertical line down from the top of the slate. "Like that."

"Can your father give us a real puppet show?" the shortest girl in the class asked, pointing in my direction. "My father can do two Mercurys racing each other, and he even makes their tails wag."

"My sister has a chicken puppet that can actually pick things up with its beak," a boy boasted. "She has to use both hands, though."

"We'll do that another day," eBeth said, displaying how well she'd adapted to her role as a teacher. "The way this game works is that I think of a word and you all take turns guessing."

"Is it educational?" Monos asked suspiciously. "We're supposed to be on holiday."

"It's just a fun game. I'll make a blank for each letter in the secret word, and when you guess a letter that appears, I'll put it in the right place. Just to make the game harder, if anybody makes a wrong guess at the whole word, I win and we start over. Oh, and with each wrong guess at a letter, I'll draw another part of the puppet."

"What if the letter is in the word twice?" Naomi asked.

"That's a very good question," eBeth said, as she drew five dashes on the bottom of the slate. "In that case I'll fill in the letter everywhere it appears. Let's do a practice run where the secret word is 'apple.' Monos, you go first."

"Apple!" the boy shouted. "I win."

The other students all congratulated their fellow on outsmarting the teacher, and eBeth waited patiently for them to get it out of their systems before adding one more blank to the row at the bottom of the slate. "Now, does anybody else want to try?"

"P?" a girl wearing her best holiday clothes guessed.

"Very good, Delphi," the young teacher said, and put a 'p' in the first, third and fourth spaces.

"Puppet," I blurted, and then retreated hastily behind the bar under eBeth's glare. "What? I can't play?"

"No!" the children all shouted together, and then dissolved in laughter at the idea of an adult playing a children's spelling game. eBeth shook her head over the latest delay, and then erased the bottom of the slate with the side of her hand and drew four new blanks.

"P!" Monos guessed, drawing a new round of admiring laughter, but this time their teacher smiled and drew a circle at the end of the vertical line. As an afterthought, she printed a 'p' at the edge of the slate.

"What kind of puppet is that?" a girl asked.

"It's just the head," eBeth explained. "If I draw the whole puppet before you guess the word, I win. David?"

"T?"

The teacher put a 't' in the last blank but she didn't look happy about it. "Harold?"

"Z?"

eBeth gave a wicked grin, drew a vertical line under the circle, and added a 'z' to the column on the side.

"Why'd you guess that?" Monos complained to his fellow student. "It's hardly even a letter."

"I like Z's," Harold defended his choice.

"Delphi?" eBeth prompted before the boys could carry the argument further.

"E," the girl said confidently. "You told us that it's the most common letter in Northern."

"I must have been right," their teacher groused, putting an 'e' in the second blank. "Abimelech?"

"A," the boy said confidently.

"Miss," eBeth proclaimed, momentarily confusing Hangman with Battleship in the building excitement. She drew an arm sticking out at an angle before adding an 'a' to the growing column of letters. "Anat?"

"I?" the girl guessed.

Another arm appeared on the purported puppet, and the 'i' went into the wrong guesses column.

"Icarus?"

The boy hesitated for a moment and then turned to his classmates for strategic help. "Should I guess another vowel?"

"It's such a messed-up language," Monos said. "It's got different words for everything."

"There are only four blanks," Naomi observed. "Lots of short words only have one vowel."

"What's another common letter, then?" Icarus asked.

"M? N?" the girl suggested.

"M," the boy tried.

eBeth drew a leg and added 'm' to the side column, but I thought she looked a little nervous, as if she'd had a close escape. "Mary?"

"N."

The third blank took the 'n' so the slate now showed a single blank followed by 'ent.'

The children huddled together for another strategy meeting, and this time they whispered to each other, occasionally glancing over their shoulders at the teacher to make sure she wasn't listening in. I was able to eavesdrop with my superior hearing, and I was surprised by the sophistication of their discussion, which led to delegating Monos as a spokesman for their concerns.

"How many more turns do we get?" he asked when the huddle broke up.

"One," eBeth told them. "As soon as I draw the other leg, you lose."

"How about eyes?" Monos demanded. "All puppets have eyes."

"He's right. Even my sister's chicken puppet has eyes," another boy chimed in. "And a mouth."

I thought they had valid points and I wondered how much flexibility eBeth would demonstrate. Truth be told, I suspected she would have made a good dictator, but I admit that my current assessment of the girl's personality had been influenced by her recent jewelry shopping advice.

"Alright, but eyes count for a single turn, and no more additions," she counter-offered.

"Deal," Monos replied immediately, tipping his hand that she'd given them more than they'd expected to get.

"Philo?" eBeth said, pointing at another boy.

"B," he guessed.

eBeth drew the last leg and put a 'b' in the misses column. "Leah?"

"D?"

Two dots appeared for eyes and the 'd' was listed to the side. The children went back into their huddle and began quietly singing their way through the alphabet."

"Is 'lent' a word?" a girl asked. "It sounds like one."

"I don't think we've had it yet," Naomi said. "Teacher wouldn't choose a word we didn't know."

"Would too," Monos argued, and I had to agree with him.

"Is 'pent' a word?" asked the same girl in a show of linguistic intuition.

"Maybe, but 'p' was used already," Naomi said. "There's still 'rent', 'sent', 'tent', 'vent', and 'went', and we only have one more guess."

"Isn't 'went' one of those strange verbs that teacher likes so much?" Delphi asked.

"You're right," Monos agreed. "How do you get from 'go' to 'went' anyway? They don't share a single root letter!"

Again I found myself impressed by eBeth's young students. While irregular conjugations were no challenge for an artificial intelligence such as myself, I imagined that the alien tourists who were certainly visiting Earth through the new portal connections must be tearing up their phrase books in exasperation and renting translation devices. The huddle broke up again.

"Naomi?" eBeth chose.

"Went," the girl said.

eBeth hesitated for a moment before putting a 'w' in the first blank, causing the children to break out in another noisy celebration. She threw me a mysterious smile, and I realized that I'd never know whether she had cheated at her own game to let the children win. It seemed like the sort of thing Sue would do, and I was coming to realize that my supposed wife and daughter had more in common with each other than I would have expected.

"Does anybody want to lick the mixing spoon?" Sue called from the door to the kitchen.

I thought that there was going to be a stampede by the way the children all started to their feet, but Spot was faster, flying in from an oblique angle and snatching the entire wooden spoon from Sue's hand on his way to the exit. The riot was over before it had even begun.

"Mark, help me bring out the sandwiches, and the cookies will be cool by the time the children finish lunch."

As I headed for the kitchen, I heard Monos asking eBeth, "What's a sandwich?"

"Like a gyro, only flatter," she told him. "You'll like it. You like everything."

Sue had outdone herself, making enough sandwiches for a small army using thin slices of home-baked bread and what looked like all of the lettuce and tomato from her garden. Throwing a white dishtowel over my arm for effect, I entered into my role as waiter for the group of young sophisticates.

eBeth had directed the children into joining a few of the smaller tables together and surrounding them with chairs so that everybody could sit together. I noticed that the students seemed to arrange themselves according to some predetermined order, and after they each took a half a sandwich and held it uneaten as if waiting for something, the reason became clear.

"Uncle John is coming to dinner," Monos announced, and all of the children passed their sandwich to the neighbor on their left. Even more surprisingly, they all seemed happy with what they got because they began munching away. eBeth took a bite from the tomato-and-mutton sandwich she'd ended up with, and her lack of reaction told me that it wasn't the first time she'd played this particular table game.

"Wasn't that a Rynxian banquet ritual?" Sue whispered in my ear.

"I don't see how," I murmured back, though I have to admit that the same thought had crossed my mind. We both watched for what would happen next.

When the slowest eater finished her cheese sandwich, Naomi passed around the bowl of small spring potatoes and each child on her side of the table took exactly one. Then she declared, "My Aunt Rachel is visiting," and the students across from them opened their mouths wide. The air was momentarily filled with potatoes describing a short arc across space, and not a single child missed the mark. Again, eBeth seemed entirely at home with the proceedings.

"That was definitely a Hanker party game," Sue whispered. "Pffift couldn't have done it better."

"And he would have known if any of his people had ever visited this world," I said. "That must mean—"

"Do you have any serving sticks?" Icarus asked his teacher. "I want to eat the way my mom taught us."

"I thought two specials a meal was the limit," eBeth replied, putting air quotes around 'specials.'

"We do three on holidays."

"I don't think we have any," eBeth said. "Mark? Do we have any chopsticks?"

"I'm afraid not," I replied, and addressed the boy. "Do you know where your mother learned how to eat that way?"

"Traveling for work," he replied, and then the conversation was taken over by an argument between Monos and

Naomi about the difference between the perfect tense in their own language and the past tense that eBeth was teaching them. Somehow the pile of sandwiches steadily disappeared despite the fact that all of the children seemed to be continuously talking.

"Cookies are ready," Sue announced, and passed me a large tray on which the dessert was still cooling. Spot chose this moment to reappear and drop a badly chewed stirring spoon at her feet. She picked it up, and for a moment I thought she was going to rap him on the snout with it, but one look at those soulful eyes and she relented, setting the mixing bowl on the floor for him to lick clean.

"So who can tell me what they want to do when they grow up?" eBeth challenged her students as they dug into the warm cookies.

"You mean after we apprentice or go to the academy?" Naomi asked.

"Like when you're my age," eBeth responded with an unconscious toss of her head.

"I want to work with my Aunt Rachel," the girl replied.

"What does she do?" eBeth asked.

"I don't know exactly, but she travels a lot and brings everybody really neat presents," Naomi answered.

"How about you, Monos?"

"I want to work for the Ferrymen," the boy declared.

"Do you mean making goods for export?"

"No, I want a job on a spaceship," Monos replied as if it was the most natural thing in the world.

"How do you get a job like that?" eBeth asked with a furtive glance in my direction to make sure I was listening. "I never see any Ferrymen around here."

The children all burst out laughing again, and I heard a couple of them repeating eBeth's comment about never seeing Ferrymen in the village as if it were the punch line to a joke.

"I've got connections," Monos boasted, and then rubbed the side of his nose in the age-old human gesture of a criminal conspiracy.

"What do you want to do when you grow up?" Delphi asked her teacher playfully, and the children laughed so hard I was afraid they might start leaking lemonade.

"I'm apprenticed to my father to be a clockmaker," eBeth told them when they finally settled down.

"When are you going to marry Peter?" the girl followed up.

"I'm not old enough yet," eBeth objected. "Besides, I don't know if I want to get married."

The boisterous children immediately fell silent, and you could have heard a feather drop, or at least, I could have.

"But you walk out together," Delphi said. "He must have asked your father for permission."

I saw that eBeth was taken completely off-guard by the sudden change of subject and might accidentally break her cover story with the wrong answer. I stepped into the breach and informed the students, "The marriage was arranged between our families when they were children. You know how that is."

Apparently they did, because the students dropped the subject without another word. Dessert was followed by a number of games whose educational value was questionable at best, unless the goal was to inculcate boys with a healthy fear of blindfolds and kissing. Then somebody suggested dancing and the children pushed all the furniture to the walls, linked arms, and exhausted themselves with going in a circle and singing in a scene that called to mind some wedding rituals from Earth.

By the time her students headed home, eBeth looked worn out, but her eyes were bright, and she came straight to me for debriefing.

"Did you catch all that, Mark? I thought that the Ferrymen were Sky Gods to these people, but Monos talked about them like they're just another employer."

"Which they aren't, at least not in the village or the towns I've visited, and Stacey hasn't seen any in the capital yet, either."

"It makes sense that Monos would know about spaceships because they're landing all the time to pick up the export goods, but he wants to work on one. I think the other children would have made fun of him if it wasn't a real possibility."

"Next time he makes trouble, keep him after class and get some answers," I suggested. "This lack of information is driving me crazy."

Eight

"What are you so happy about?" Helen asked as we parked our bicycles in front of the miller's cottage. "You've been grinning like the Cheshire cat the whole ride out."

"It's this new saddle that Sue gave me for Ferrymen's Day," I confessed, a bit embarrassed that my satisfaction with the gift was so obvious. "The old one was too narrow."

"Why didn't you buy a replacement yourself?"

I frowned. "I'm not sure, really. The saddle that came with the bike wasn't optimal for the pelvic structure of my encounter suit, but it wasn't doing any permanent damage that I'm aware of."

Helen nodded in understanding. "I'm that way with money, too. Cheap."

"I'm not cheap. I was just trying to avoid waste."

"What did you do with the old saddle?"

"Chopped it up with an axe," I said, unable to suppress my sense of satisfaction. "Listen, Helen. The folks who live around the village think that you're a bit wild because of the way you ride your bicycle. Let's try not to give them anything new to gossip about today."

"I'll be good, but I'd guess it has more to do with my dancing than my biking."

"What dancing?"

"I'm always out at night to watch for the Originals, and when I hear the music from a barn dance, I just can't resist dropping in. Don't look at me like that. I was going to put it in my report."

I swallowed my response, and instead asked, "You're sure you've done this before?"

"I was collimating my own home-built reflector telescopes when you and Sue were still learning how to do floating point math," Helen said. "Did you bring props?"

"All the measurement instruments I own," I replied, removing the optics-related tool box from the exchangeable rack on my bike. "The miller's daughter is probably here, and she's studying astronomy in the academy, so she may be familiar with the process."

"Then she'll be impressed with the results," Helen said, and knocked on the cottage door.

"It's not the results I'm concerned about, it's the effort. If you do it ten times faster than she's used to it will look suspicious."

"Don't worry. I'll pretend to use your instruments and I can fake doing math on a slide-rule with the best of them."

The door opened and we were greeted by the miller's wife.

"Mark. Helen. Thank you for coming out during the holiday week. Sophus is so excited about his new telescope that I couldn't stop him from sending the dog to see if you were available."

"It worked out fine, Palti. My niece wouldn't have been available next week."

"Is that so," the miller's wife said, and I couldn't help suspecting that she would have preferred waiting. "Well, Sophus and Athena will be thrilled that you're here. He's in the new shed out back."

"We'll just head around then," I answered for both of us. As I guided Helen to the path that ran between the cottage and the mill, I told her, "I suppose he didn't pay for a folding tripod so he can't bring the telescope inside without disassembling the mount. Millers make good coin but he's a bit—whoa!"

"Is that thing a telescope or a hollow log?" Helen asked, but I could tell that she was impressed by the tube sticking out of the shed's roof, the half that wasn't covered with canvas stretched over curved ribs. The overall effect reminded me of the time I saw a convertible creeping down the road back on Earth with the roof stuck half-open. Alerted to our presence by his dog, Sophus emerged from the new building almost immediately, his daughter in tow.

"Thank you for coming, Mark. And this must be your niece who I've heard so much about."

"Helen," my team member introduced herself. "And whatever you've heard about me is an exaggeration. How was I supposed to know that the pole wasn't for dancing?"

"It was for dancing," Athena said. "We tie long ribbons to the top and dance in circles around it. Nobody had ever seen what you did before and the boys are still talking about it. Don't you get dizzy spinning around upside-down like that?"

"I'm out of practice, actually, but it's kind of like riding a bicycle. You were there?"

"The marriage celebration was for one of my oldest friends. Did you know the groom?"

"I was just out and about."

I decided to jump in before the exchange went any further. "That telescope looks like it belongs in an observatory, Sophus. I'm surprised you…"

"Could afford it?" the miller completed my unfinished thought. "The lenses and mirrors are from an orbital factory. According to Athena, microgravity is the ideal environment for making optical parts."

"I'm just repeating what my instructors say," the girl admitted with a slight blush at hearing her father repeating terms she'd just finished explaining to him. "They're also much less expensive than the parts made on our world, and the import authority finally reached an agreement with the lens-grinders guild last month. I sent mom a letter as soon as I heard about it, and she put in one of the first orders to the telescope maker that sponsors our class."

"I'm surprised I didn't see an announcement in the Engineer's Journal," I said. "They do regular reports about additions to the import list."

"The Engineer's Journal is great for technology and classified ads but their news items lag a couple months," Athena told me. "It's just not a priority with them."

"That makes sense. So, I invited Helen along to help with the collimation because she has more experience with reflector telescopes than I do."

"Athena took care of tuning everything already," Sophus told me proudly. "We would have been up all night stargazing if not for Bright Moon getting in the way."

"Oh. I thought the note said you needed help with the setup. Were you just inviting me out for a look?"

"It's the tracking mount," the miller's daughter told us. "It was supposed to come ready for operation but I can't even wind the spring."

"You really are building an observatory," I marveled. "I've never seen a tracking mount on a backyard telescope."

"The business that makes them contracted with our academy to test a homeowner version and I was one of the students assigned to the project. They offered to loan students the used pre-production units in return for regular performance reports. I couldn't resist."

"Let's take a look at it," I suggested, and we all followed the girl into the observatory shed. Once inside, I could see that the roof had more ribs than the typical convertible and the overall shape when the roof was closed would closely mimic a dome. The walls were numbered, prefab panels, which explained how Sophus, who wasn't known for his building skills, had erected it himself. But the tracking mechanism was a thing of beauty that must have cost as much as a couple of new bicycles.

"The crate had a note about seeing the included instructions but there weren't any," the miller griped. "Athena has hundreds of hours of experience using the device but she's never set one up."

Back on Earth, I would have stealthily downloaded the instructions from the manufacturer's website or raided their internal database if a public document wasn't available, but neither option was available on Reservation.

"They probably forgot the instructions because it's not a retail package, but I'll be back at the academy long before we could get a new set sent out by mail," Athena added. "Everything looks the way I remember, but I never paid much attention to all those gears. And I don't know where the counterweights go because this isn't the same telescope as the one I used at the academy."

"I'm sure we can work it out," Helen told her. "Why don't you look at the mechanism, Mark, and I'll figure out the counterweights."

"It's too bad eBeth wasn't awake when we left," I said. "She's getting good at visually analyzing gear trains."

"Does it look alright?" Sophus asked anxiously just a few seconds later. "I was so excited when it came that I might have gotten a bit careless prying the planks off the crate. I thought it would be packed in something to prevent shipping damage, but it was only secured at the base with a few bolts through the bottom."

"That's alright," I assured him. "I'm pretty sure I see the issue and it's a good problem to have. They've installed wedge-clips and locking collars throughout the gear train to prevent shipping damage. Normally there would be a diagram highlighting the locations of all of the safety devices. Did you check the inside of the lid?"

"I'll look now," Sophus said, squeezing past me and out of the shed.

"I want one of these," Helen declared as she installed the counterweight on the spindle. "We could build a little observatory on the roof of The Eatery."

"Numbered," I announced, holding up a wedge-clip. "Six of thirteen. You keep track of these, Athena, and we'll know when we have them all."

"I can't thank you both enough," the girl told us. "The telescope is great, but so many of the objects my dad wants to view are moving too fast to track manually because the field of view is so small. I tried to get him to change to the lower power eyepiece, but he wants to see everything at maximum magnification."

"I'm curious to see this tracking mount in action myself," I told her as I continued to strip out all of the shipping safeties. "I imagine it requires a bit of practice to get the angles and the speed correct."

"Yeah, it's not super-easy to use, but getting the speed right is the main thing. As long as the object you're viewing isn't zipping right through the field of view, you can adjust the vector on the fly with that little knob."

"It's a brilliant piece of engineering," I told her. "The only thing that's missing is a camera mount."

"Shhh!" she cautioned me. "Dad doesn't know they make them and Mom doesn't want him finding out. It's not so much the cost of the camera or the photographic plates but she worries about developing. One of her cousins got hooked on taking nature photographs and their whole house stinks like chemicals."

"See how the tube moves," Helen suggested to the miller's daughter, who put the telescope through its full range of motion.

"It feels perfectly balanced now," Athena reported. "How did you know the exact position for the counterweight?"

"I'm a good guesser," my team member replied.

"You were right, Mark," Sophus said, returning to the hut with a large diagram. "This was tacked to the inside of the lid, but it's just a picture, no written instructions."

"A picture is worth a thousand words," I stated, and wasted a microsecond wondering if it was too late to get credit for the phrase on this planet. "Let me see if I missed any locking collars."

To my chagrin, it turned out I hadn't spotted the largest one, which I had mistaken for a flywheel. Once it was removed, Athena counted up all the pieces of packing hardware and checked the total against the drawing.

"That's it," she said. "I think the only thing left is to connect the drive rods to the universal joints on the mount's base."

"This part is just like the power train that moves the clock hands you see on towers," I explained as I made the connections. "Even though the telescope has much more mass than clock hands, these drive rods turn so slowly that there's not much force involved."

"I've already learned to keep my hands off the tube while I'm viewing," Sophus said. "The slightest touch and I lose whatever Athena has focused on for me."

I used my all-in-one pocket screwdriver to secure the drive rods to the universal joints on the tracking mount and wound up the mainspring that provided the motive power for the gear train before stepping back.

"I'll leave the rest to the expert," I said, nodding to the girl.

"I probably won't be able to focus on anything with the sun so high, unless Phobos is visible," Athena cautioned us, disengaging the clutch that allowed her to swivel the telescope on the mount without fighting against the gear train of the now-attached tracking mechanism. Then she sighted through the low-magnification spotter, searching for the hurtling ball of rock that would no doubt burn up in the atmosphere in the next ten million years or so if somebody didn't wake up and nudge it into a higher orbit.

"Got it!" Athena exclaimed and reengaged the clutch. Then she pulled out the actuation knob that allowed the mainspring to set the whole gear train into motion and moved around to where she could look through the eyepiece while reaching the controls for the tracking mechanism with her left hand. Her experience showed as she adjusted the speed and balance between the different drive shafts by changing the gear selectors, and then fine-tuned the speed by adjusting the tension on a slipping disc drive. "Look now, Dad."

As Sophus carefully worked his way around the periphery of the crowded shed to the eyepiece, I remained intent on the gear train, which was performing the work of an analog computer. It was a fascinating combination of mechanical technologies that I'd never seen used in this particular combination. I immediately saw several ways in which it could be improved, but the design had clearly been driven by price considerations, and that it worked at all was a testament to the engineers.

"Is that really Phobus?" the miller asked in awe. "Are you sure you didn't focus the telescope on Widow's Peak by mistake?"

"It's just a chuck of rock in space, Dad," Athena reminded him with a laugh. "Tonight I'll show you the star system the Ferrymen rescued us from."

"We can see that far?"

"Not with the naked eye, but I think this reflector has enough magnification. We look at old Sol through the academy reflector sometimes, and the light we see probably left there before the Ferrymen started making their visits. Isn't that strange to think about?"

"Weird," Helen agreed. "The speed of light is a pain."

"That's why we should get portals," Athena said casually, the first time I had ever heard portal technology referred to on this planet by anybody who wasn't on my team. "But the Ferrymen don't want to lose their monopoly."

"The Ferrymen have a monopoly on portals?" I asked, knowing that those lazy aliens couldn't build a portal if their lives depended on it, but curious to learn how an academy student viewed the galaxy.

"Not on the portals, on us," the girl replied, as if it were the most natural thing in the world. "We're a valuable resource and they don't want to share us."

"Come and look, Mark," Sophus said, tearing himself away from the eyepiece. "Athena, go get your mother. She should see this too."

I would have preferred to continue the conversation, but I could hardly countermand the miller in his own observatory, so I stepped around Helen and looked through the eyepiece. My greater sensitivity across the spectrum combined with integration to lift the signal from the noise allowed me to pick out a few of the brighter galaxies that bracketed the moon. The smoothness of the relative motion between these objects only increased my admiration of the tracking mechanism and Athena's skill as an operator. "You try it, Helen."

My team member eagerly took my place, and I could see the left hand of her encounter suit twitching as she imagined herself repositioning the tube and looking for some of her own favored celestial objects, namely comets. I doubt she could have held back if it was night, but the brightness of the local sun was no joke.

"Look who I found," Athena said, as she approached with her mother and an older man in tow.

"Saul," I greeted the county safety inspector, stepping out of the observatory shed to do so as it was rapidly running out of space. "What brings you back out here during the holidays? Another Original sighting?"

"I came to see my old pupil's setup," he replied. "I used to tutor Athena in astronomy back when she attended the village school, but she's moved far beyond me now."

"He's just teasing," the miller's daughter told me. "Saul used to work at the spaceport doing real astrophysics stuff, and he tutored the local kids during summers when he took a month at his camp on the lake. People used to bike in from all over the county to look through the telescopes he set up each year."

"Young man's work. Now I'm happily retired into a part-time public service job and I get to meet all sorts of interesting types."

I noticed that his eyes shifted to me when he uttered that last part, and it seemed that he intentionally avoided the more common expression, 'all sorts of interesting people.' But maybe he had recently come from an up-close and personal encounter with an Original.

"You never mentioned working at the spaceport," I said, carefully keeping any tone of accusation out of my voice even though it was beginning to feel like somebody was setting my team up. "You must know all about advanced alien technology that would make the local telescopes look like children's toys."

"Not at all," Saul replied. "I'm far from an expert in optics, but the waves that make up the visible light we see can only be magnified so much by lenses. For the size of the reflector, I imagine that this instrument is every bit as good as any optical telescope in the League."

There, he had said it out loud. The locals were aware of the League of Sentient Entities Regulating Space, even though we'd only known about the existence of the reservation worlds for six months. However the Ferrymen were managing their humans, it was plain that they weren't keeping them in ignorance of the greater galaxy. I was beginning to see that my ban on team members asking leading questions during our first six months on the planet had cost us a great deal of knowledge.

"I've always been interested in aliens," I said to Saul, which was one-hundred percent true for a change. "If you have the time to stop by The Eatery, I'd love to pick your brain, and there's an extra bed if you want to stay over."

"I'm looking forward to it," Saul replied. "I've always been interested in aliens myself."

Nine

I heard a funny growl behind me and stopped with my hand on the front door latch.

"What is it now, Spot?" I asked the dog without turning around. "You've been out three times already this morning."

Spot growled again, and then gave a sharp bark. I turned around to see what looked like a leather chew-toy, which had obviously fallen out of his mouth when he'd barked, tumbling down the stairs. When it came to rest at my feet, I realized that it was an old-fashioned leather messenger's tube decorated with a fair amount of slobber.

"You shouldn't be chewing on that," I scolded the dog as I bent to pick it up. "Did you bring it in from outside? You'll have to show me where you found it."

Spot barked impatiently before executing a tricky turn while still on the stairs and heading back up. I removed the plug from the leather cylinder and drew out the tightly rolled message, hoping there would be enough clues to decipher who it was intended for before the dog had found it in the road or stolen it off a porch. To my surprise, it was a note from my mentor asking me to meet him at League headquarters immediately.

I ran down to the basement and grabbed the project I'd been working on in my spare time for the last three months, and then back up two flights of stairs, where I found Spot sitting in front of the empty closet where the engineers had installed our permanent portal entrance. I used one foot to ward off the dog as I slipped into the closet, and then I sent the command code and selected the portal reserved for Observer teams at the League headquarters. My mentor was there to greet me when I stepped through.

"I hope I didn't keep you waiting," I said apologetically. "There's no knowing how long Spot was chewing on that cylinder before he delivered it."

"Just a few minutes," he replied in spoken English, matching his language to the human encounter suit which, for some obscure reason, he had chosen to embody a portion of his mind while serving as Library's representative on the League's executive council. "You haven't reported in since your initial assessment, and none of your team members have seen fit to submit status reports during their smuggling trips."

"I don't know anything about that," I told him honestly. "With my active sensing suite turned off, I don't even know where my team members are unless they're standing right in front of me."

"It must be the first time you've ever been so isolated from other sentients," my mentor said, and his voice expressed a note of fatherly concern I'd not heard from him in hundreds of years. "How are you and the team coping?"

"Now that you mention it, we all seem to be developing a few personality quirks," I replied. The strangeness of the admission hit me even as I heard my own words, reminding me again that conversations with my mentor went better when we abstained from high-speed communications. "Perhaps it's a side effect of the human encounter suits."

"Are you offering a formal report presentation of a data crystal?" my mentor asked, indicating the jeweler's box in my left hand that I'd forgotten I was holding.

"This is for you," I said, handing it to him. "I could never figure out a gift to buy to show my appreciation for all of your help so I made you this."

"Are you hinting that I should retire?" he joked after opening the box. Even though my mentor was a master at guarding his true thoughts, I could read from the expression on the face of his encounter suit that he was deeply impressed by my gift of a gold watch. "I'm not familiar with all of these indicators."

"Date, month, and the inset shows leap years, where they have to add a day to keep the calendar in sync with the seasons. You can set alarms based on the time and date out to a year, which is an invention of my own, and if you pull out that knob it functions as a stopwatch."

"What's this little slider for?"

"It's also a minute repeater," I told him proudly. "When you pull out the slider, the watch chimes the hours and quarter hours so you can tell time in the dark. Well, not you, obviously, but there's no electrical lighting on reservation so it's the kind of thing that comes in handy at night. The chiming mechanism added over a hundred and fifty discrete pieces to the watch, including two hammers."

"Can I wear it in the shower? I've found that these encounter suits require frequent cleaning."

"It should be waterproof to a hundred meters," I confirmed. "I haven't actually had the opportunity to test it, but if you should ever go scuba diving…"

"I'll be sure to send you any data," my mentor said as he slid on the wristwatch. "Did you make the band as well?"

"No. That's a standard flexible band for men's gold watches that's manufactured on Reservation for export. There's a spring in every link and you need specialized tools to work on it, so let me know if you need the band resized."

"This will do just fine. Thank you, Mark. It's the nicest gift I can remember receiving."

I was so taken aback by his excessive praise that I hurried to deflect it with a question. "So what's so urgent that you had to pop through the portal and draft the dog into bringing me a message?"

"I'm getting pressure from the council to fill them in on what you're doing."

"How much do they already know?"

"Only that the engineers opened a new portal for the Observer service to investigate possible abuses by a League member. The council is recessing for the long break today, but you know how paranoid some species are about Library's actions. I expect they'll push for full disclosure as soon as we reconvene."

"And when will that be?"

I couldn't help grinning when my mentor looked at his watch before replying.

"Just over two months of your local days, the exact timing depends on how many rounds the Goonpal tournament goes. Please try to have a final report ready as quickly as you can."

"Maintaining radio silence to conceal our presence from the Ferrymen has been a major operational obstacle, but things have started opening up the last week," I told him. "One of the planet's natives walked into my bar a couple nights ago and ordered an ale."

"Was there a duck involved?"

"What?"

"I assume you're telling me a sentient-walks-into-a-bar joke."

"No, this really happened."

"According to your initial assessment the planet's native intelligent species was being treated in accordance with League rules, but had only reached a minimal level of tool usage, such as fishing insects out of holes with a stick. Now you're saying that they socialize with villagers and participate in the economy?"

"It came as a shock to me as well. The locals are all schooled to respect the privacy of the natives by never addressing them and simply turning away in case of chance encounters. Such meetings rarely occur because Originals primarily move about at night and there aren't any gas streetlights in the small towns and villages. But I just found out that the indoor gardens the humans plant in their larger buildings are set aside as space for the Originals should they care to drop in and observe."

"And this native spoke to you in the local language?"

"Not exactly," I hedged. "I've always encouraged eBeth to continue with her education and I thought that a stint of teaching might pique her interest. I convinced her to take a teaching job at the village school."

"Teaching English," my mentor immediately guessed.

"We passed it off as the language from the Northern continent but I'm beginning to suspect that they're on to us."

"And this native spoke English to you."

"I don't think his vocal chords could reproduce human sounds, but there's no question that my visitor could understand the spoken language, and he wrote his replies on a slate."

"And what do you make of this?" my mentor asked, performing the single eyebrow raise that I had yet to perfect after nearly four years inhabiting a human encounter suit.

"I haven't been on as many missions as some observers and I didn't specialize in alien anthropology, but that Original would have fit right in on any barstool in the League. Our conversation wasn't long, but given the little he did say, I'd be willing to bet that the natives are at least as intelligent as the human colonists."

"But they produce no buildings or artifacts."

"None that we've found, though I've heard of cliff art attributed to them. It's on my list to see some."

"I think you had better make another trip to the Library archives," my mentor advised. "I haven't changed my access code."

"You're authorizing me to make a deep data dive on your credit?"

"We're both aware that something out of the normal is going on here and I don't want to be caught off guard." He looked again at the watch I'd just given him and said, "Two forty-one. I have to run or I'm going to be late for a subcommittee meeting."

"On Reservation time?" I asked skeptically.

"I created a translation algorithm based on the sweep-hand movement while we were talking. There's no point in my resetting the watch given the different units in use here, and I'll know what time it is on Reservation if I need to get a hold of you. Don't wait so long before you contact me the next time."

"Understood," I said. "Thanks again for the library code. This will be invaluable."

He waited politely while I reprogrammed the portal destination for Library, and I was in the act of stepping through when he called after me, "Give my best to Sue, and congratulations on your engagement."

Before I could even begin to formulate a response, I was hundreds of light-years away in the Library waiting room, with the atmosphere from the League's headquarters pouring out of my mouth as I'd forgotten to purge my system with the sudden change in plans. How could my mentor possibly know about my accidental engagement? Was there a double agent on my team?

I pushed away the thought as I sat down on a bench and decanted from my human encounter suit, which remained frozen in place. On uploading my mind to the vastly superior infrastructure of Library, I felt like a human might on growing a pair of wings. In my case, the whole experience was being paid for on my mentor's credit.

During my only previous deep dive into Library's archives, I'd almost lost myself in the seemingly infinite data that implied a level of causality and connectedness between all events that could be dangerous to the sanity of a young artificial intelligence. This time I was better prepared, and I struck out immediately for the scientific survey data from the volume of space which contained all three of the worlds that the Ferrymen had populated with humans transported from Earth.

When I dove into the data about the planet my team was investigating, I was surprised to find that it had been visited by a scientific mission less than fifty thousand years ago. Since that time, the ecosystem of the two continents occupied by humans had been overrun with flora and fauna the Ferrymen had imported from Earth, but something was missing, and I tried another query.

The information you've requested requires Level 63 authori-zation.

I'm acting for Library's representative on the League's executive council, I replied to the head librarian. *I'm using his code.*

Our League representative hasn't changed his access code in several millennia and therefore explicit authorization is required.

He's in a meeting hundreds of light years away, I argued. *Who else can confer Level 63 authorization? I've never even heard of it before.*

The board of trustees, Library's representative to the League, and the head librarian. None of the board members are available.

So that's the way it was. I'd heard that the head librarian wasn't above extorting information from patrons to increase Library's store of data, but I'd never experienced it first-hand. Come to think of it, I suppose the head librarian never thought I had any knowledge worth acquiring.

What do you want in exchange?

Your initial report indicated the presence of native megafauna predating the arrival of the Ferrymen and humans. What is the basis for that assessment?

Information from the humans. I have one team member assigned to studying the natives, but they are nocturnal nomadic gatherers who create few artifacts for study. My mission is undercover so we are hardly in a position to start archeological digs to—

I'm aware of the limitations placed on your mission, the head librarian interrupted. *The answer to your query is that there was no megafauna on the world at the time of our last survey mission.*

That's not possible, I protested before I could catch myself. Communicating at the speed of thought has its drawbacks, and I had been spoiled by four years in my human encounter suit which gave me time to think. *It means the Originals are not native to the planet.*

Keep me informed, the head librarian said, and withdrew from the conversation.

My primary purpose in coming to Library had been to learn whatever I could about the evolution of the natives on Reservation, but now it turned out they were recent arrivals. Could they be the survivors of a crashed ship or stranded test subjects from a failed intra-dimensional portal experiment? In that case, Library might have records of their species existing elsewhere.

I checked the usage fees for Library's universal image-matching search and almost blacked out. There was just no way I could spend that much of my mentor's credit on what might be a wild goose chase. Instead I designed a much more limited query, looking for correlations between the Ferrymen and a 3D memory of the so-called Original who had visited my bar. It came up blank.

I was about to transfer back into my human encounter suit and return to Reservation when something about my search query reminded me of the Hankers and the way they mixed and matched body parts. Paul had completed our antenna array and was monitoring the direction of the M13 star cluster for Pffift's message but we hadn't heard a word. Back on Earth, the Hanker had improvised a coded message to me about his intentions by claiming that his sixteen-hundred and seventy-ninth birthday was coming up and he would send an invitation. I'd assumed that the prime number reference to the Arecibo message had been the payload, but had he doubled down on his meaning?

A quick look through the current public records yielded Pffift's birthday in Hanker terms, which I converted first into Earth years and then into Reservation years. Bingo! If the alien was half as clever as I was giving him credit for, he'd be contacting us in just over two weeks, local time.

A few minutes later, I stepped out of the second floor closet door and was surprised to find Spot still waiting. Then I noticed the little scraps of leather all over the carpet and realized that he had thoroughly chewed up the messenger tube that I had carelessly left behind.

"Hey, Mark," eBeth said, emerging from her bedroom. "What are we doing today?"

"You're awake early," I couldn't help commenting. Her stated ambition for the school break had been to sleep late every day, and checking my internal clock, I found that she was up at her usual time.

"Yeah. I tried to stay in bed but it just didn't work. There's something wrong with this planet."

"It's the lack of artificial lighting," I told her. "When none of the moons are up it's pitch black outside, and even during the nights when they're all visible at the same time, the reflected light isn't that much brighter than a full moon back on Earth."

106

"I have candles."

"Back home you had electric lights, a smartphone, a laptop, and the Internet," I reminded her. "It's a wonder you got to sleep at all."

"This is okay too," she said as if it was occurring to her for the first time. "It's kind of nice in the morning. The air smells fresh."

"I don't have any work scheduled because of the holiday," I told her. "I was planning on riding my bike out to the hills to look for cliff art. How about packing a picnic lunch and inviting Peter along?"

"He's working," she replied with a pout. "Paul left for the provincial capital with Stacey, and Peter says that even though the machine shop is officially closed, he has to stay around in case of emergencies."

"It's nice that he takes his responsibilities so seriously."

"His priorities are messed up," eBeth retorted. "Is Sue coming?"

"She's staying home to handle the lunch business so that the former owners can take time off," I told her as we headed downstairs to the kitchen. "Helen will come with us if I can find her."

"How about Spot? You can leave your toolbox home and he can ride on the rack."

"Or he can run alongside."

Two hours later, when Spot's barking bought our attention to a narrow fissure in the cliff face that led into a sort of crevasse that was illustrated with the most astounding art I'd ever seen, I had to thank eBeth for convincing me to let him ride.

"It's beautiful, sort of," the girl said. "But spooky too, and kind of—" she broke off and looked away. "Don't try to follow the blue lines all the way to the end or you may get dizzy."

"I think I know what this is," I said, though it didn't make any sense. "I saw something similar once when I attended a presentation about stability issues with the portal network. It's a map of sorts, like for the circulatory system of a body, but in this case, it's showing portal connections in this galaxy, and beyond."

"I thought you said you didn't know much about how portals worked and that they don't function between galaxies."

"Intra-dimensional portals will operate anywhere in this universe. It's just that at great distances, our engineers haven't solved the problem of keeping the end-points lined up. And everything I know about portals is from a public lecture series I attended on Library. I just have a hard time imagining another artificial system that would imitate this architecture."

"So where's the branch for this world, or for Earth?"

Spot jumped up against the wall on his hind legs, a rare exertion for the dog, and scratched at a colorful nexus with one forepaw.

"Down, Spot," I barked at him, and with an irritated look over his shoulder, the dog dropped back to the ground.

"He didn't hurt anything," eBeth said. "Whatever the Originals used to color all these lines must be pretty tough. You know, I think there are actually channels engraved in the rock and filled in with something."

I went over to take a closer look at the area Spot had scratched, and other then a small "x" on top of what was likely a major portal intersection if my theory about the diagram was correct, there wasn't any sign of damage. I took some time making mental images of the cliff art for memory, taking extra care since I suspected Library's head librarian would put a high value on the information.

eBeth and Spot had finished their picnic lunch by the time I completed the job, and I was disappointed to find that that the basket was empty.

"What's the matter, Mark?" eBeth said. "You look like somebody kicked your puppy."

"I just thought Sue might have packed something for me," I admitted.

"Since when do you care about food? You used to complain that eating just made for a hassle cleaning up."

"I don't need food, of course, but I've noticed lately that chewing and swallowing give me an odd sense of satisfaction. Especially things that crunch."

"Like carrots and celery?" eBeth asked innocently.

"You ate them?"

The girl reached under her jacket and brought out the paper-wrapped package. "I was just teasing."

Sitting with the girl and the dog munching on a carrot and letting myself enjoy the aesthetic of the cliff art without worrying about its meaning, I felt strangely pleased with myself. One of these days I really had to run a full self-diagnostic on the encounter suit, but not today.

Ten

"You look tired," I said to eBeth when she joined me in my basement workshop. "Did you stay up late playing board games again?"

"Spot kept me up half the night making funny noises. I think he was trying to teach himself how to whistle."

"Dogs don't have the right mouths or lips for whistling. Maybe he's sick."

"I can bring him by the apothecary shop and ask Kim to check him out," eBeth offered. "Do we have any jobs today?"

"All of those parts I bought in bulk from the scrap dealer need cleaning."

"I mean real jobs, fixing stuff."

"Cleaning is a big part of the job, eBeth. It's a big part of most jobs."

"I think I'll just take care of Spot first."

"I may as well come along," I said. "You go find the dog and I'll meet you out front."

I carefully put away the tools I'd been using and moved my current project to the storage area of the workbench so it wouldn't be in the way if a rush job came in. I could hear a number of people moving around in the dining room above my head even though we weren't open for breakfast and I wondered if Sue had visitors over. Given my ban on communications when we weren't face to face, I had suggested leaving each other messages on slates, but for some reason she found my logic annoying.

When I met eBeth and Spot out front, the dog greeted me with an elaborate yawn, a sure sign that he was up to something. Oddly enough, he looked well rested, and comparing his body language to the reference images I kept in memory, I got the impression that he was rather pleased with himself. We crossed the road to the apothecary shop and found Kim in a deep discussion with a woman at the counter.

"We can come back," I offered, not wanting to interrupt a consultation.

"We were just finishing up," Kim replied, pushing a small paper sack across the counter to her customer. "Remember, there are no miracle cures, but if you follow the instructions to the letter you'll feel much better by the end of the week."

"How much do I owe you?"

"There's no charge today."

We stood aside as the woman left, her hood pulled up around her face so I didn't even recognize her. The bells on the door jangled as she exited and Kim turned her attention to us.

"Is something bothering you, eBeth? You look tired."

"I got to sleep late is all. We came to ask you to take a look at Spot."

"Is he sick? I'll get my bag and be right over. Justin is upstairs working on something so just give me a minute to tell him to come and watch the counter."

"There's no need for that," I told her. "We brought— where is he?"

"You know, I'm not sure he came in with us," eBeth said. "I remember crossing the road and opening the door, then we saw the woman at the counter and I wasn't sure whether to enter or not."

"Hold on a sec. I'll check," Kim said. She looked down at something on her side of the counter, fiddled around for a moment, and reported, "Spot didn't come in with you. What's wrong with him?"

"He was whistling half the night," eBeth said. "It was weird."

"Maybe he just has a tune stuck in his head from listening to Mark singing those ballads behind the bar every night."

"But I distinctly remember Spot brushing up against my leg as we entered," I protested. "And what do you have hidden under the counter there that you're looking at?"

"We set up a camera to monitor the road out front," Kim said. "Don't get excited, Mark. Anybody who notices will take it for a 'My Life' recorder, and Justin ran a shielded cable to the display. Come and take a look."

I followed eBeth around the counter and saw that my team members had installed a poorly camouflaged Faraday cage with an LCD display inside that was cycling an old screen-saver of a fish tank. The whole deal was powered by an inverter hooked to a car battery which they must have been manually recharging through their encounter suits.

"Why isn't the bubbler making any noise?" the girl asked.

"It's not a real bubbler," Kim told her, and directed an infrared command at the box. The fish tank suddenly transformed into a wide-angle shot of the road in front of the apothecary shop, providing an excellent view of The Eatery in the background. The video recording showed eBeth, Spot, and I crossing the road, and at the last minute, the dog peeled off as I followed the girl into the store.

"I don't get it," I said. "If I could plug into that thing, I could display from my own memory when I looked down and—it's not there anymore!"

"You probably flushed your buffer without thinking about it," Kim said. "I only hold a second or two worth of streaming video myself. Who has the memory to waste?"

"Me, apparently, though I run heavy compression. I got into the habit of holding onto the last couple hours since I started working on clocks and watches. Some of the craftsmen building them are pretty idiosyncratic."

"What's that mean?" my apprentice asked.

"They feel driven to do things their own way," I explained. "If you're not paying close attention when you disassemble some of these clocks it will take you forever to figure out how to put them back together."

"Oh. Could I run my laptop in something like that?" eBeth asked. Behind her, I shook my head 'No' at Kim, who unfortunately was looking the other way at the moment.

"Sure, but it really cuts down on the brightness and you'd have to get one of us to keep recharging the battery for you. On second thought, it wouldn't work because you don't have built-in infrared so there would be no way to issue instructions."

"I don't get it," I said to Kim, hoping that eBeth wouldn't think of asking why she couldn't just be inside a Faraday cage with the laptop. "Of all the things you could smuggle onto Reservation, why did you feel you needed a security system?"

"It's not for security. A few months after we took over the shop, I happened to be returning from a house-call when I saw a boy approach our door and then turn away. I caught up with him at the edge of the village and he finally admitted to being afraid he wouldn't have enough to pay. Apparently the old apothecary was in it for the money."

"So now you monitor everybody who approaches the shop and if they don't come in you go after them?"

"Justin and I split up the area around the village so that between us, we recognize everybody who lives within walking distance," Kim explained. "If somebody who really looks like they need help doesn't come in, I make it a point to ride out on my bike."

"What do you say to them?" eBeth asked.

"It depends on the time of day and where they are. Sometimes I pretend to be lost or that I'm just stopping by to fill my water bottle. If I see bikes out front I may pretend to have a flat and ask to borrow an air pump."

"So you're monitoring the video all the time?" I asked.

"No. We just fast forward through it in the morning and the evening. That reminds me," Kim said, and I saw her eyes emitting another stream of infrared commands. "I meant to come over and tell you about this."

The video was much darker than the previous shot, though the camera she was using didn't show the graininess of low light environments. An Original strolled into the field of view, glanced over at the apothecary shop, and did a comic double-take. He took something out of his mouth, walked directly towards the camera, and the last thing visible was his hand with something shiny stuck on the tip of a claw looming large before the picture was lost.

"It took me five minutes and a half a bottle of alcohol to clean that gum off the lens," Kim complained. "I hope this doesn't become a habit."

"How could he have spotted the camera so easily?" eBeth asked. "I've never noticed it before."

"I thought about that. It's shielded for radio frequency emissions, but it would show up as a hot spot if the Originals see into the infrared, which explains their night vision."

"Got any other bits of smuggled technology you've been meaning to tell me about?" I asked.

"Nothing leaps to mind," Kim said. "It's funny to think that when I was on Earth, I couldn't make enough portal trips back to civilized space to pick up medical supplies. Now that we're here, I realize that Earth actually makes some pretty useful products, at least for humans."

"We did manage by ourselves quite a while before you came along," eBeth said. "What kind of stuff do you import?"

"I bring in hydrocortisone by the bucket and mix it with aloe vera for a burn cream that I'm selling by mail order. If you have time this morning, I could use a little help packing orders."

"It beats cleaning old gears in a dark basement."

"Fine," I said, figuring out that I'd been abandoned by both my dog and my supposed daughter in the space of five minutes. "I promised Paul I'd check in on Peter every couple days to see if he needs a hand with anything. Any messages?"

"Humph," eBeth said, turning her back. It was the first indication I'd had that things weren't going well between them. Kim made a face at me followed by a lip-zipping gesture, so I swallowed my question.

An agonized yell came from just outside and I raced for the door. A heavily loaded farm wagon was parked in front of The Eatery and somebody was standing by the back wheel, cursing like a Phoenician.

"Get it off me, get it off me," Hosea shouted when I emerged from the apothecary shop. The wagon must have slipped back and trapped his foot below a wooden wheel when he was reaching over the sideboard to retrieve a melon from the bed, probably a gift for me. I threw myself under the wagon and pushed up on the rear axle, like doing a one-ton bench press, and the farmer pulled his foot free.

"Thanks," Hosea said in a surprisingly calm voice. "I was on my way to the canal and thought I'd drop off a few melons on the way. That'll teach me not to set the brake."

"Can you walk?" I asked him. "Let's get you to the apothecary and let her take a look at it."

"Oh no, I'm fine," he insisted, thrusting a melon at me and climbing back onto the wagon seat. "I guess my toe was in a bit of a rut there so the foot didn't get crushed at all. Just scared me, being unable to move."

"I really think…" I began, but the oxen threw themselves forward the moment Hosea cracked the whip, and the wagon rumbled off in the direction of the canal weigh station. Something made me look back the opposite way and I saw Saul lounging in front of the boot maker's shop, engrossed in the county broadsheet that was the closest thing to a daily newspaper in our area. I thought about confronting him with my suspicions, then decided to let it pass and headed for Paul's machine shop.

Peter was working a treadle-powered lathe to turn the shaft of what looked suspiciously like a crude MacPherson strut when I entered. At first I thought he was modding a bicycle, but then I noticed new mounting plates on the carriage in the shop's bay space that looked like a racing model.

"Any problems since Paul left?" I asked.

"Not with the shop," the teen replied, allowing the lathe to spin down. "Demetrius stopped in earlier and picked up the order of gear bodies for chain hoists I've been working on all month and he said they were as smooth as anything he'd seen."

"I've noticed the improvement in your work myself. I'm just not sure how it will translate when you get back to Earth since machining is all done with computer controls now."

"I'm not worried about that," Peter said, turning towards me, but not quite meeting my eyes. "Could I ask you something?"

"You can ask me anything."

"About eBeth."

"Oh. Well, you can ask, and if it's not appropriate, I'll tell you."

He picked up a heavy chunk of cast iron that looked like a crude steering knuckle and began filing it while he talked to have something to do with his hands.

"It's like this. You know that party eBeth had for her students on Ferrymen's Day?"

"I was there."

"Right. And eBeth said that you told the kids that she and I were promised to each other as children."

"They were asking her awkward questions and I was afraid she would say something suspicious. You know that this is a traditional culture and they take courting rituals very seriously."

"I don't have any problem with it at all. But when eBeth told me about it, I said, 'That's cool,' and she got mad at me."

"Why?"

"I'm asking you."

"About women?"

Peter nodded. "Paul used to help me with this stuff, though for some reason his advice isn't nearly as good as it was back on Earth."

"That's because back on Earth he was probably sending your questions to Stacey over our private channel and then giving you her answers." I took a moment to gather my thoughts. "Listen, Peter. When I have a problem with Sue, I ask eBeth, and if she's not around, I take her advice about following my intuition."

"You have intuition?"

"It's not very good. eBeth's advice was to do the opposite of whatever I think makes sense and it's worked out pretty well when it comes to Sue. Relationships between artificial intelligences are nothing like human relationships, but there's something about living in these encounter suits that make us vulnerable to your cultural norms. I don't know how else to explain it."

"So how can I find out why eBeth's angry at me?"

"Well, my first instinct would be to ask her, so that's obviously not an option. Maybe she wants a ring."

Peter stopped filing and stared at me. "I never even thought of that. Thanks, Mr. Ai."

"You're supposed to spend three months of your salary," I told him. "If you're short, I'll be happy to loan it to you."

"Like an engagement ring?" he croaked. "I thought you just meant she liked jewelry."

"You're the one who brought up the two of you being promised to each other by your parents."

"Which you invented," he said, backing away from me as if I represented a threat. "No offense, Mr. Ai, but I think I'll wait for Paul to get back, or maybe I'll ask Sue."

"You don't want to marry eBeth?"

"Of course I do, someday. But she never even knew her dad and she gets scared by relationship stuff."

"Oh, maybe you have a point," I allowed. "I told you I'm the wrong one to ask for advice."

Peter didn't have much to say after that, and I'd already lost eBeth to the mail-order business for the morning, so I decided to return to my workshop and get the batch of old parts I'd purchased cleaned up in anticipation of rebuilding the turret clock for the Ferrymen Temple. I was just about to enter The Eatery when Kim called to me from across the road and then disappeared back into her shop. When I got there, she just motioned for me to come behind the counter.

"Did something happen to eBeth?" I asked.

"She's upstairs helping Justin fill jars," Kim said. "Watch the video."

The fish tank screensaver again transformed into a view which included The Eatery across the way. A wagon rolled into the frame with two men sitting on the bench, Hosea and Saul. The former hopped down, a small trowel in his hand, and rapidly dug a little hole in front of a rear wagon wheel while the county safety inspector moved to the front of the wagon and produced a pair of apples.

Hosea slipped the toe of his boot into the hole, tossed the trowel in the wagon bed, grabbed a melon, and nodded to Saul. The two oxen lunged forward just enough to take the apples, and the safety inspector jogged out of the picture. Then Hosea opened his mouth, and a second later, I ran into the frame faster than any human had the right to move and did my wagon-lifting trick.

"Oops," I muttered.

"They set you up," Kim said. "I don't know what that wagon weighs, but it's more than a human should be able to lift."

"I could blame it on adrenaline."

"It was a test, Mark, and you passed, or failed, depending on your point of view. They have to know that you aren't human."

"Funny, I've never felt more human in my life."

Eleven

I was just about ready to head downstairs to my work-shop for the night when I heard the telltale sound of a recumbent bicycle skidding to a long halt in front of The Eatery. In deference to Paul's carefully cultivated affectation for alcoholic beverages after a long day's work, I drew a tankard of ale, and then bypassed the default thermodynamic settings for the hands of my encounter suit to lower their temperature and put a chill into the beverage. By the time he was seated at the bar there was frost on the pewter.

"You're back much sooner than I expected," I greeted him. "I'm assuming that the Ferrymen didn't catch you snooping around or you would have broken radio silence to request extraction."

"Ferrymen," Paul snorted, and took a long pull at the chilled ale. "Not bad, but it wouldn't kill you to smuggle in a few cases of single malt Scotch, just for team morale."

"Or you could ask Kim to modify the inebriation algorithm to produce the same effect from drinking water."

"Where's the fun in that? Your problem is that you're cheap."

"Let's not go there right now. What did you and Stacey uncover?"

"You can drop the ban on radio frequency emissions," Paul stated with absolute certainty. "Nobody is listening."

"Are you sure? The Ferrymen may be employing shielded receivers, and without an active detection grid, we don't know what they may have in orbit."

"There's nothing. No Ferrymen, no satellites, no advanced technology beyond the 'My Life' editing stations and the cargo transports. Haven't you noticed that we never pick up any ground control chatter?"

"The Ferrymen are trying to keep this world's existence a secret so it makes sense they would handle all of their routine communications with point-to-point systems like lasers."

"There's nothing, Mark. They don't land ships at night because there are no homing beacons or lights at the spaceport. The cargo transports come and go on a clockwork schedule. There aren't any Ferrymen on this world or on the ships. I double-checked."

I found myself wishing that I had smuggled in at least one bottle of Scotch because I suddenly felt the need for a stiff drink.

"They're running interstellar ships on autopilot?" I asked in disbelief. "That's a union beef. If word gets out, their ships will go unloaded at half of the spaceports in the galaxy."

"They have pilots. Human pilots. Human crews. The whole operation is run by humans, and none of them are tasked with monitoring the spectrum." Paul drained the remains of his tankard and slid it towards me. "Once it became obvious what was going on, I gambled on slipping a bug onto a newly arrived transport."

"You might have asked first," I grumbled.

"I used one of ours," he said, by which I knew he was referring to Library surveillance technology, which was probably beyond the Ferrymen's ability to detect in any case. "I got eBeth to camouflage a couple for me before we left."

"Are you serious?"

"She's really good at using little bits of thread and feather to make fake insects that look sort of like the real thing," he reminded me. "If she and Peter were really trying to catch fish, the river would be empty by now."

I let the fishing comment pass since I didn't understand what he was getting at. "So you infiltrated a zero-emissions bug, recovered it, and downloaded the recording."

"Which I'll be happy to pass to you as soon as you lift the ban," he told me.

"What was the double-check you mentioned?"

"I might have been pushing it a bit with that one, but I was confident," Paul admitted. "You know those entertainment visors the Ferrymen never take off?"

"It's kind of sad," I acknowledged.

"I hacked into one of the 'My Life' editing stations and altered it to transmit a phony free subscription signal on the frequency used by the visors. There's no way any Ferrymen would have passed that up."

You win, I transmitted. *Send me the data dump.*

While Paul cooled his second ale, I devoured the bug's surveillance video at my maximum speed. Not only were humans crewing the Ferrymen cargo ships, they were preferentially using manual control systems.

"They probably know more about running those ships by now than the Ferrymen," Paul said, accurately reading my mind. "What I can't understand is why the humans are sticking to the covenant when they must know that no-body is watching."

"None of this makes any sense," I muttered, pouring myself a glass of local brandy even though I didn't care for the sweet taste of the stuff. Then I powered on my active sensing suite for the first time since we landed on the planet and sent a ping to remotely activate everybody's location transponders. All of my team members were where they were supposed to be, and their encounter suits showed the slight movements that were pre-programmed to simulate breathing, except Helen's.

"Turn on your sensor suite," I told Paul.

He looked up from his ale in surprise. "It's been so long that I forgot I even had one. Funny what you get used to."

"What do you make of Helen's signal?"

"Stationary. Too stationary. But maybe she's observing an Original and doesn't want to give away her position."

"Possible," I allowed, and then messaged her directly with the news that I had lifted the emissions ban.

"Whuh?" she responded several long seconds later, and if I didn't know better, I would have said that her trans-mission had a sleepy harmonic to it.

Are you alright?

Everything is fine. I'm just – tired.

We don't get tired, Helen. Is your encounter suit experiencing power problems?

Wait, I'll run a self diagnostic, she replied

"What's going on?" Paul asked with a slight slur in his pronunciation, and I noticed that he had chugged through his second ale.

"Helen is running diagnostics," I told him. "You might want to ask Kim to recalibrate that inebriation simulation. The alcohol shouldn't be hitting you so fast."

"It's more efficient this way," he replied, and leaning over the bar, refilled his own tankard. "You know, I don't think I've run a self-diagnostic since we came to this rock."

"I haven't either," I admitted. "I've been meaning to though."

We both straightened up and stared at each other, apparently having reached the same conclusion.

"It must be the radio silence," Paul said. "Living in encounter suits among a native population always takes a toll, but by cutting off most of our non-human senses, you accelerated the process."

"I'm running a self-diagnostic now," I replied, and fell silent as the high-level routine temporarily took over the encounter suit and began comparing the default settings with the current working values.

Everything passed, Helen reported. *According to the black box, it appears that I've been experiencing regular suspensions of processing, but they are logged as voluntary.*

You've been napping, Paul told her. *I caught Staccy doing the same thing when she came back for the holiday. We checked in with Kim and she gave us a simulated caffeine algorithm she's been working on.*

And nobody thought it was important enough to tell me? I demanded as my encounter suit came back online.

It's still in Beta, Paul explained. *You know how careful she is with medicinal algorithms.*

I didn't want to worry you, Kim chipped in without my having added her to the chat, which meant that either Paul or Helen had brought her in. *Sue thinks that you're over-worked.*

This is the easiest mission I've ever been on, I protested. *And for what it's worth, my self-diagnostic came back all green.*

Don't test the encounter suits, test yourselves, Kim advised. *We were going to bring it up at the next meeting, but Justin and I failed the standard Library rationality diagnostic.*

"The poor fools," Paul said to me out loud so that the others couldn't hear him. *It's a trick test, Kim, you fail by taking it. Artificial intelligence that questions its own sanity is insane by definition.*

There's nothing wrong with any of us, I hurried to reassure them, and checked my mission-commander interface for the first time in months. *Kim, you and Justin have warning flags set. See if you can wipe them, and if not, I should be able to do it with a command override.*

Are you sure about this, Mark? Justin joined in the conversation. *Even if the test is trivial, it's there for a reason. Maybe we should portal out to Library and have ourselves evaluated.*

That's the second part of the test, Paul informed them. *If you turn yourself in you've gone completely nuts. Think about it.*

I agree. Helen contributed. *I knew an AI on an Observer mission who turned himself in after going native and he's been the one under observation ever since. What does Sue think?*

"Oh no!" I groaned when I realized that I'd been making critical decisions without even soliciting input from my second-in-command. *Sue. I've just lifted the ban on radio frequency emissions,* I sent to her private channel. *I'm here with Paul and we were having a bit of a discussion about our recent behavioral quirks. A few of the others have already joined in.*

Is this about Justin and Kim failing their sanity test? Sue responded immediately. *I told them not to worry about it. We're just feeling the effects of isolation from any meaningful information network, not to mention the limitations you put on our communications.*

I know, I know. It turns out the Ferrymen weren't even monitoring.

Hey, it's great to hear from you guys, Stacey said, meaning that Paul had invited her to the chat and that my whole team would now be showing up like hot spots if anybody was watching the planet from orbit. *Who failed the sanity test? I have a team alert in my message queue but it doesn't specify.*

Justin and I, Kim told her. *I guess our resets removed the personal identifier but not the general warning.*

There, I said, having located the override and electronically signed a lengthy disclaimer about clearing sanity alerts. *Is everybody clear on what's happening?*

I don't see eBeth and Peter on the location grid, Sue said, and the amplitude of her transmission suggested panic. *What could have happened to them?*

They don't have transponders, Paul reminded her. *They're not human—I mean, not artificial intelligence.*

Wow, we're pretty messed up. Helen commented, the understatement of the year.

Now that everybody is back in contact, I'm sure we will start reverting to our normal selves, I transmitted hopefully. *I want you all to take the rest of the night to summarize the data you've been saving up, and then we can pool our knowledge to be prepared for the big push.*

And what will that be? Justin inquired.

Contact, I said confidently, even though the idea had literally just sprung to mind. *If the Ferrymen have granted the humans full autonomy and stepped back from direct supervision of this world, our original mission is no longer necessary.*

Pitching the humans on League citizenship won't make the Ferrymen happy, Paul pointed out. *And what about the Originals?*

We need more information there, but it's obvious that they're sentients, so they'll have to be included. The question is whether the humans and the Originals should be approached as a joint civilization or individually.

"Tell me the truth," I said to Paul after the other team members disconnected from our electronic chat. "Did you smuggle in the components for a detection grid?"

"You know I like to be prepared," he replied, which I took as a yes.

"Are the ground units deployed?"

"Did you think I was riding around on that bicycle every night for the sake of exercise? I started activating the grid the moment you lifted the ban but it's going to take a while to tune. Without any satellites for reference, the only way to fix the remote locations is through triangulation."

"Is your inertial guidance disabled? Why didn't you just fix the points when you placed the elements?"

"You know that the coverage of a ground based grid depends on spreading the net as widely as possible. I have units positioned all over the continent."

"You couldn't have ridden that far!"

"I had them delivered."

"To who?"

"Myself. I rented warehouse space at the main canal terminal in every province. It's amazing what you can get done by mail on this planet."

"So you *do* know where all the units are."

"Only to the resolution of the canal system maps. They're not bad given that the routes were laid out by surveyors using line-of-site optics, but when you consider the detection grid is scanning light-hours out, small errors add up."

"But it's just an early warning system," I said. "It's not like you need to handle targeting for weapons systems."

Paul fiddled with his tankard and didn't reply.

"I said, it's not like you need to handle targeting for weapons systems," I repeated.

"Just a particle beam projector," he admitted. "What if I spot an incoming asteroid? If I'd been on Earth sixty-six million years ago we'd be talking Dinosaur right now."

"What do you need me to do?" I asked tiredly.

"You ride your bike out into the hills and I'll head back towards the capital. As soon as there's a good distance between us, I'll have each one of the remotes send a timing signal, and then I can compute the exact locations from the difference in delay."

"Don't we need to synchronize our watches first?"

"You really have gone native," Paul said with a laugh. "Have you forgotten that our encounter suits are crystal-locked to Library time?"

I had forgotten, but I passed it off with a chuckle and headed out back to grab my bicycle. By the time I'd wheeled it around to the front of The Eatery, Paul was already out of sight. Two of Reservation's four major moons were full enough that our riding bicycles on the road wasn't a dead giveaway that we could see in the dark, but we also counted on the locals being home in bed.

I rarely saw humans riding their bikes after sunset, and those who were out usually pedaled slowly, keeping within the feeble beam of light cast by a sealed reflector lantern. In forested areas, it was easy enough to stay on the road simply by watching the clear ribbon of sky overhead, but bicycles were so expensive that most of the locals were unwilling to gamble on damaging them in a silly night-riding accident.

For the first time in six months, I reached out with all of my active sensors, including millimeter-wave radar, and almost fell off my bike. An Original was silently loping through the fields parallel to the road, casually leaping over fences and irrigation ditches as he kept pace. Yes, the resolution of my night imaging is more than sufficient to pick out anatomical features on a running anthropoid in the dark. How long had the Originals been following me, and were they tracking the rest of my team as well?

Paul, I sent. *I'm under observation.*

Pedal faster, he replied. *I lost my tail a minute after I left the village.*

That's not the point, I transmitted. *I want to know how long this has been going on.*

Can't turn back time, Mark. I've had the feeling that somebody is watching me the whole time we've been here, but I wrote it off to paranoia.

Since when does artificial intelligence suffer from paranoia?

You really should have paid more attention to pop culture back on Earth. I'm activating the first unit. Transmit your absolute receive time to me.

For the next hour I followed Paul's instructions, helping him bring the detection grid online and calibrating the results. Coverage wasn't perfect because three-quarters of the world's surface was ocean and he'd only managed to ship a couple of units to the northern continent, but taking the planet's rotation into account, we would get a reasonably complete picture of local space at least once a day.

What's your stalker doing, he sent when we finished.

Keeping his distance. I don't think he knows that I'm onto him.

Assuming he follows you back home, do you want me to nab him?

I considered the plan for a moment and then rejected it. *No. Let's let them think that they're in control of the situation. If we panic them, they could go to ground and the seven of us would never find them.*

Okay. I'm returning to the village and I'm going to take the gag off my antenna's receiver. I'm getting tired of having to manually connect to check if there's been any action. It's primitive. Next time you insist on radio silence I'm going to rig the receiver with an alarm or a flare.

Twelve

"That's the last time I give my students a pop quiz on their first day back from vacation," eBeth declared, throwing herself onto the bench where Spot was snoozing. "Ow! When are you going to buy a couch?"

"I'm worried about spillage," I told her. "Did your students all fail?"

"They cheated," the girl complained. "Who cheats on multiple choice tests? I was so disappointed that I pretended not to notice when everybody around Naomi began copying from her and passing their papers around, but I still had to send Monos to the back of the class because he was repeating the answers out loud and distracting everybody. Then he started acting like a complete maniac."

"You mean he threw a tantrum?"

"It was more like watching one of those crazy street people back home. He was holding up his paper and talking to the indoor garden like a bush was going to give him the right answer. I was so freaked out by the whole thing that I snuck out the front exit and went around to the back of the auditorium so I could stick my head in the door and see what he was doing. And you know what?"

"He was reading each question and all of the possible answers—"

"He was reading each question and all of the possible answers—" eBeth continued before my words registered. "How did you know?"

133

"There's an Original hiding in the garden auditing your class. His English is very good, at least as far as listening and literacy goes. He isn't able to speak, though, so he must have been shaking a bush or giving some other sign when Monos hit the correct answer."

"And you were going to tell me this when?" eBeth growled at me.

"Sue said it might upset you," I lied, throwing my second-in-command under the bus in the same way husbands on Earth blame their wives. "He seemed very nice."

"Does this Original have a name?" she demanded icily.

"Art, though he might have made it up on the spot. They aren't actually original, by the way. At least not to this planet." The girl's eyes grew even colder, if that was possible. "I was going to tell you soon," I concluded feebly. "I've had a lot on my plate."

"If Monos knew about the Original hiding in the auditorium's garden then everybody else had to know about it as well," eBeth said, after a few minutes of giving me the silent treatment, during which I did my best to look remorseful. "There's no way that boy could keep a secret."

"It seems that the humans on Reservation build indoor gardens in their large meeting rooms to give the Originals an opportunity to observe," I told her. "My mistake was in assuming that the greenery was there for health reasons or as a sweetheart deal for the glass blowers to help them sell window panes."

"So I'm not only pretending to teach Northern to my students but to an alien as well!"

"I think he knows it's not Northern," I told her, figuring I would get all the bad news out in one shot. "I suspect that the villagers know it's not Northern as well. As a matter of fact, I'm pretty certain that everybody has us pegged for aliens."

"But I'm NOT an alien," eBeth protested. "I'm as human as the villagers. More human, if being born on Earth counts for anything."

"There aren't any Ferrymen on the planet," I said, rushing to get it all out. "The humans run the whole show and keep to the covenant for their own reasons, though I have the feeling we'll be finding out soon enough."

"Is that everything?"

I reviewed the recent events in my mind and added, "I visited Library. Somehow my mentor knew about Sue's engagement ring, and I figured out that Pffift will be here any day."

"I certainly didn't tell your mentor about the ring if that's what you're implying," eBeth said, but I detected a hint of obfuscation in her speech pattern.

"You did tell somebody," I hazarded a guess.

"Just because it was funny. I mean, come on. I think you knew all along what I was doing and you just wanted somebody to blame in case Sue rejected you. I even asked how much you earned the last three months before picking out the ring."

"That did ring a bell, but without Internet access—"

"You could have checked your copy of Wikipedia."

"Your turret clock will be here in a few days," I said.

"Smooth," eBeth mocked me. "I never saw that subject change coming. And since when is it my turret clock?"

"It's your apprenticeship graduation project," I told her. "Technically, you don't meet the time-in-service guidelines, but I'm counting the three years you helped me on Earth and giving you credit for sixteen hours a day."

Spot barked a short warning from out front, and a quick scan showed me that the headmaster of the village school was approaching The Eatery with two other humans, one of whom I recognized as the county safety inspector from the unmistakable radar signature of the bronze star on his belt. The female was a mystery.

"Are you forgetting to tell me about something that happened at school today?" I asked eBeth.

"Oh, right. The headmaster said to tell you he'd be stopping by. He apologized for not making an appointment but he knows that you come home at lunch to take me out on your afternoon repair jobs. I told him you wouldn't mind."

"Hard to believe he's that anxious about the clock," I said with a frown. "This could turn out to be sticky. Maybe you had—"

"—better stay here and make sure you don't do anything stupid," eBeth completed my sentence.

Considering I was going to suggest that she sneak out the back door, her guess wasn't even close. Before I could crow about it, The Eatery's front door opened and the delegation trooped in, with Spot bringing up the rear.

"Joshua, Saul," I greeted the headmaster and the safety inspector at the entrance to the dining room. "I hope none of you have had lunch yet. It's a little late and the kitchen is between shifts, but I'm sure eBeth and I could manage something between us."

"We've already eaten," the headmaster assured me. "I don't know exactly how to put it, Mark, but this isn't a social visit."

"Is eBeth in trouble?" I asked, focusing my attention on the woman who accompanied the men. She carried herself like Lieutenant Harper, which reminded me that I was due to make a smuggling run to Earth myself. "My daughter was raised on the northern continent, you know, and they do things differently."

"I do know," the woman replied. "My name is Hilde and I'm the customs officer for the northern continent stationed at your provincial spaceport. Saul asked me to come."

"I hope I haven't been breaking the law by mail-ordering parts from other provinces," I said, mainly to buy time for eBeth, who had turned beet-red when Hilde mentioned being from the northern continent. None of the visitors as much as cracked a smile at my weak joke. "Why don't the three of you come in and have a seat?"

Saul grunted his assent and led the others to the table I indicated, confirming my suspicion that he was the one in charge. I gave eBeth a head tilt towards the exit, but despite the fact that she was obviously battling off a panic attack, she elected to stay. I tried a different head tilt on Spot, who interpreted it correctly and moved in close to the girl to offer emotional support.

"We'll come right to the point, Mark," the headmaster said. "We know that you and your extended family and friends aren't from this world."

"I've been called a lot of things in my life but this is the first time somebody has taken me for an alien," I fibbed, at the same time silently alerting my team that we'd been made. "What led you to this bizarre conclusion, Joshua?"

"The day you arrived through your temporary portal outside of the village, a shepherd happened to be recording an authenticity video of himself watching his sheep," the headmaster replied. "He didn't notice your arrival because he was facing the wrong way and he's a bit deaf, but an editor at the spaceport saw your group appearing out of nowhere in the video's background and alerted the administration."

"When did this allegedly occur?" I asked, clinging to the idea that we might yet talk our way out of it. Mass hallucinations wouldn't cut it as an excuse since the evidence was on video, but maybe I could convince them that the images were ghosts from a previous recording that hadn't been fully erased.

"The spaceport authorities notified me within a week of your arrival. The opportunity to have a native speaker from Earth come in and teach to the children was too tempting to pass up," he said, turning to eBeth. "I'm sorry we deceived you into believing we thought you were teaching Northern, but we wanted more time to assess what your group was doing here before showing our hand."

"I forgive you," eBeth said immediately. "Actually, I felt bad about teaching a language the children may never get the chance to use. But if you already knew I wasn't teaching Northern, why bring her?" she asked, indicating Hilde.

"Customs is the closest thing we have to a global security service on this planet," Hilde replied, her answer suggesting that she was familiar with policing on other worlds. "Saul thought it would be a good idea to have a senior representative along, and I happened to be available."

"So why are you telling us this now?" I asked, eBeth's confession having rendered pointless any further attempts to cling to our cover story. My main concern was that other aliens were involved and that Paul had been wrong about nobody monitoring the radio frequency spectrum. "Are you acting in place of the Ferrymen?"

"We wanted to confirm that you were artificial intelligence before contacting you," Saul said. "The Ferrymen may not be the only aliens who transported a population of humans to another planet. You might have been industrial spies from a reservation world set up by a different species."

"The Ferrymen may have moved humans to more than one planet," I said, curious to find out how much they knew.

"They seeded three worlds with humans, as I'm sure you already know. Now that I've answered your questions, I'd appreciate if you could tell us your purpose in coming here."

I was a bit taken aback by the directness of his approach, but with our cover blown, there was no reason to sow further confusion.

"My team's previous mission was to evaluate Earth for membership in the League, with which you're obviously familiar. On discovering that the Ferrymen had set up reservation worlds for humans, we were tasked with assessing your condition."

"To offer us membership to the League?" Saul asked cautiously.

"That's above my pay scale," I told him. "The Ferrymen are already members of the League, so our initial brief was to make sure they weren't violating Sky God rules on this world."

Strangely enough, all three members of the delegation breathed a sigh of relief at my answer, leading me to conclude that they didn't want to be invited to join the portal network. I was still phrasing my next question when eBeth asked, "How did you know that Mark is artificial intelligence?"

"Little things," the headmaster told her. "We've all taken turns testing your math skills, physical abilities such as strength, reaction time and night vision, and none of the young men who've seen Helen dance believe that it's humanly possible."

"But it is," eBeth told him. "I've already told her she should teach a class."

"Have her talk to me. It's a shame we don't get more use out of the building outside of school hours."

"Maybe the Originals have a full schedule of classes in the middle of the night," I suggested, trawling for whatever information they might have been holding back.

"The natives are solitary creatures," Saul said, which told me that he wasn't aware they were as alien to the planet as the humans. "The Ferrymen prohibited us from interfering with them, though our scholars who study the League's laws suggest that this was overly cautious since the Originals are obviously intelligent enough to make their own decisions."

"Our turn," Hilde said. "Our security at the spaceport reported an alien insect flying around inside a ship and raised the alarm about a potential invasive species. Attempts to quarantine the bug failed, but one of the crew members who saw it thought it was likely artificial."

"Was he a fisherman?" I asked.

"How did you know?"

"I guess that was my fault," eBeth said. "I made some insect disguises for mobile bugs and I used my imagination."

"Very impressive for artificial intelligence," Hilde said.

"I'm as human as you are," eBeth blurted out before I could stop her. "So is Peter."

"From Earth?" the headmaster asked, and received a head nod from the girl in confirmation. "That's fine, then. We don't expect any competition from that direction."

"What's wrong with Earth?" she demanded.

"We don't have portal access ourselves so this is all second-hand, but according to reports in the galactic media, the planet is technology-crazed. Even if there are still people in poor areas with the skills needed to compete with us, they'll be the first to leave your planet for cushy jobs in the galactic service industry. Your world scored an eight on the League's long-term planning scale."

"Out of ten?"

"A hundred," I told her. "Don't feel too bad. You scored above average for energy, even if you spend most of your time running in circles."

"While our sponsors are a bit lazy," Joshua said with a chuckle. "Are there any species in the League who do less with more?"

"You'd be surprised. At least the Ferrymen wander around and find other sentients to earn them profits. There are a number of fully automated civilizations at the bottom of the scale who can't even be bothered to communicate with the rest of us anymore. In fact, I doubt anybody would notice if they died out and were replaced by their robots."

"If I could return to the subject at hand," Saul said politely. "Although our people have been traveling the galaxy in Ferrymen ships since we took over distribution for our goods hundreds of years ago, none of us could risk using the portal network for fear of being detected. We're told that the filters can see through any physical disguise."

"That's true, although now that Earth has joined the League, you could pass as, uh, Earthlings," I said, with an apologetic glance at eBeth for using the term she disliked. "What I don't understand is why you seem intent on keeping your existence a secret from the rest of the galaxy, especially when you're doing such good business."

"The Ferrymen are the ones doing the business," Hilde reminded me. "We're just their humble workers."

"Why don't you take over?" eBeth demanded with the impetuosity of youth. "If you're making the goods, flying the spaceships, doing the marketing—are the Ferrymen good salesmen?" she interrupted herself.

"No," the headmaster told her. "The only thing the Ferrymen are good at is ferrying. They used to dump our excess production on the galactic equivalent of flea markets and accept whatever was offered. It wasn't until our people took over distribution that we started getting fair prices for our goods."

"How much do the Ferrymen let you keep?" she asked.

"You mean, what's their cut?" Joshua smiled. "Fifteen percent."

"It still seems an awful lot for doing nothing," eBeth objected, though it was clear that her estimation of the local humans had taken a quantum leap.

"That's brilliant," I said, putting fifteen and eighty-five together. "You're taking advantage of all of the Ferrymen's grandfathered agreements for slots at spaceports."

"Correct," Hilde said. "And that's just the tip of the iceberg. Our sponsors have reciprocal trade agreements in place with hundreds of species, which save us a fortune on import tariffs. Our economists have calculated that if we joined the League ourselves, it would cost us almost a third of our gross profit."

"And that's after the extraordinary expenses involved in setting up to do galactic business on our own," Saul added. "The populations and production of our three worlds are still growing, but without the Ferrymen to front for us, we'd just be bit players struggling to arrange for access to markets and discounted shipping."

"So you ARE dependent on the Ferrymen," eBeth argued, apparently unable to accept the synergistic relationship between the two species. "If they'd allowed you to develop your own advanced technology, you could be building your own interstellar cargo ships by now."

"It's not that simple," the headmaster told her patiently. "The advanced species of the galaxy are jealous of their technical know-how for several reasons, and one of them is self-preservation. Have you ever thought about what they all have in common?"

"The portal network," eBeth answered immediately, and began ticking off items on her fingers. "Weird customs for eating. Space stuff. A bizarre sense of humor."

"All of those things are true, but you're missing the most important point," Joshua said, glancing over at me as if seeking permission to tell her. I shrugged, figuring if Sue chose to give me a hard time about it, I could claim the headmaster misinterpreted my reply. "Every advanced species out there has survived their innovations. They didn't accidentally turn their suns into black holes, kill themselves off with biological experiments, or create weapons so terrible that a simple argument could result in planetary destruction."

"You're saying they won't share their technology to protect us?" she asked skeptically.

"To protect themselves," I told her. "The League can step in to stop wars but we can't prevent them from starting. All of our members maintain defensive forces, and history has taught us that sharing technology inevitably weakens our positions."

"But the portal system…"

"Library installs and operates the League's intra-dimensional portals for a small fee. Their principles of operation are a closely guarded secret."

eBeth frowned, and I could see that she needed a little time to absorb this latest confidence. Turning back to Saul, I said, "I'll have to report this meeting to my direct superior. Is there any specific message you want passed along?"

"Your customer service is a disaster."

"Excuse me?"

"We've been trying to make contact for hundreds of years."

"You must be going about it wrong," I protested. "It's not like Library has a direct line or a galactic mailing address."

"My point exactly."

Thirteen

I felt guilty about slipping over to Earth while eBeth and Spot were sleeping, but technically, Observers are forbidden from using our dedicated portals for personal gain and I didn't want to get either of them in trouble. As soon as I arrived in the basement office of my old restaurant, I connected directly to the Internet and began catching up on the news, though it was difficult to know what to believe. While cross-checking newspapers around the world against each other, I swapped my Reservation clothes for jeans, a T-shirt and sneakers.

Nobody paid me any particular attention when I emerged from the 'Employees Only' door at the top of the basement stairs, even though the dinner rush was in full swing. The lieutenant was sitting in his usual spot next to the waitress station at the bar, nursing an orange juice. You have to admire a man who stops drinking alcohol the day he takes ownership of a restaurant.

"Evening, Mark," the lieutenant greeted me, without the slightest sign of surprise. "Run out of slide rules already?"

"How'd you guess?" I asked, taking the seat next to him and gesturing to Donovan. "Coke," I told the bartender. With any luck it would dissolve the raisins stuck to the sides of my holding tank and save me a flush cycle.

"Couple of boxes from UPS came for you. I left them outside the storeroom door since you have a way of showing up within a few hours of when they arrive. If I had known ahead of time I'd be acting as your shipping agent, I would have talked you down on the price of this place."

"You didn't pay me anything," I reminded him.

"Then there's that," he acknowledged. "So, tell me something. If slide rules are allowed on this new world you've gone to spy on, why do you need to import them from Earth?"

"We're not spying and it's a question of cost and availability. I'm giving the slide rules away as advertising and it would have taken months of back-and-forth correspondence to get them manufactured on Reservation. Here I can upload a few files to the Internet and they show up within a week."

"Seems kind of like cheating," the lieutenant commented.

"It is cheating. How's the franchise operation going?"

"Our trademark application for 'The Portal' got rejected and it turned out that my partners wanted to use the restaurants to sell weed. I've been a cop for too long to wrap my brain around that one. Besides, I've been working on a better business idea."

"Is it legal?"

"It's not illegal," he replied. "The law hasn't caught up with any of this intra-dimensional stuff yet. Did you know that people have been suing each other in your League's courts?"

"It's your League too, now that Earth is a member. And I can't imagine any circumstances under which our courts would have jurisdiction. They only deal with interstellar matters and trade disputes between species where the contract didn't specify a venue."

"From what I heard, their backlog is like a hundred years, so lawyers do it for leverage in negotiations. The filing fee is so small that it's worth putting in a complaint just to muddy the legal waters. I know a process server who's cleaning up."

"Thanks. I'll have to let Library know and see if there's something we can do to stop it," I said. "So what's your business idea?"

"Tourism."

"You've got a bit of competition there, Bob. Promoting inter-species tourism has been the main business of the League for the last fifty million years, give or take."

"I'm talking about intra-species tourism," he said. "Keeping it secret using your portal in the basement."

"You want to compete with the airlines?" I asked, looking at him the way that eBeth and Sue look at me when I say something stupid. "Do you picture me standing around the Tokyo airport, saying, 'Hey, buddy. Want a cheap trip to America?' Aside from the fact that my team members and I are the only ones who can work this portal, it operates independently of the regular portal system. It's only good for reaching worlds with an observer team—"

"Now you get it," the lieutenant said as he watched my expression change. "I imagine that there are quite a few people on Reservation who would like to see the old country. From what you've said, it's been a couple thousand years for most of them."

For a moment, the potential almost overwhelmed me. Humans on Reservation had no practical way of reaching Earth. League citizens accessed the public portals with crystals that also served as unique identifiers, allowing Library to properly route transfers and keep track of everybody's whereabouts. Earthlings hadn't been issued crystals yet because it was an expensive undertaking and the national governments had no interest in paying. The portals on Earth were all linked to the same waystation where temporary crystals were issued to travelers for a small fee and a large deposit.

"How did you think that up?" I asked the lieutenant.

"Sitting on this barstool and watching the TV experts desperately trying to say intelligent things about places they've never even visited. There's a guy on that channel— who am I thinking of, Donovan?"

"The wormy guy who's always talking about tentacles?"

"Yeah, him."

The bartender scratched his head. "I just think of him as the wormy guy who's always talking about tentacles."

"The point is—what was I talking about?"

"Bringing in tourists from Reservation," I told him. "I'll have to discuss it with the rest of my team. I think a couple of them are trying really hard to keep their noses clean this time, and we're talking about a pretty big violation of our employment terms."

"Take a good look around the storeroom before you head back," the lieutenant suggested. "I'm going to start making contacts with travel agencies to see what kind of packages we can offer. From what you've told me, I think that Greece and the Middle East will be popular destinations."

"I'll think about it," I said, and finished off my Coke before standing. "Thanks for the drink, Bob. I can't believe how much I used to complain about the radio frequency noise on this world. Living on Reservation for six months with no input beyond what my eyes and ears could bring in almost drove me nuts."

"When are you going to take me there for a visit?" he asked.

"That would be a bit tricky right now, but I promise you'll be the first."

My new shipment of custom slide rules was right where the lieutenant said they would be, and following his suggestion, I popped my head in the storeroom to see how he was managing things. I didn't see any of the standard brand names from the restaurant supply business on the boxes, so I started taking a closer look at the labels.

Half of the boxes in the storeroom had been shipped to one or another of my team members, which meant they had all been sneaking through the portal and placing orders over the Internet. I peeked at the packing list on a box addressed to Sue and discovered that she was risking her neck for baking supplies. Oh well, the least I could do was carry it home for her.

I took the back stairs down from the closet portal to the kitchen and dropped off the smuggled ingredients. My active sensor suite warned me that there were late night guests in the dining room, so I wasn't surprised to find Art sitting at The Eatery's bar waiting for me. I was, however, bowled over to find that the four Originals sitting in a line were identical twins, or quadruplets, whatever the proper term might be.

"Art," I spoke in their general direction as I slid in behind the bar. "Can I get you the usual?"

One of them held up all three fingers on one hand and the middle finger on the other. I chose to interpret it as a counting technique and began pulling four ales from the tap.

"To what do I owe the honor of this visit?" I asked as I delivered the first tankard.

"We need to talk," the one I assumed was Art printed on a slate. Then he opened his mouth and made that loud static noise that tickled the edges of my spectrum analyzer. On a hunch, I offered an audible carrier signal of my own, and within a fraction of a second, he matched it, and then began modulating his tone with a simple binary code that I easily resolved into English.

I see you've lifted your ban on radio frequency communications, Art sent. *Is this form of communications acceptable to you?*

I'd prefer straight RF without the audible tone if you can manage it, I replied, all the while thinking that I'd run into some odd sentients in my life, but these Originals took the cake.

For a while, he replied on the low AM radio band. *It's a bit tricky in this body.*

You're wearing an encounter suit? That would explain a lot of things.

No, this is my body, or rather, these are my body. Part of it. I have a few hundred more iterations wandering around the area.

A naturally occurring hive mind? Listen, I know that you aren't native to this planet.

When did I say I was? We're here on vacation.

You're going to confuse me if you swap back and forth between first person singular and plural, I warned him.

150

I'm not the only one of my kind here, Art said. *All of us are occupying multiple bodies due to storage constraints. I imagine you have the same problem with the artificial form you're wearing.*

It was a tight squeeze, I replied, a bit embarrassed that I was able to fit my life experience into the available capacity. *Are you claiming to be artificial intelligence?*

Gee, what tipped you off? Art inquired acerbically, and his clones elbowed each other like schoolboys.

You aren't League citizens, I hazarded a guess, at the same time putting out munchies for the clones as I recalled Art's fondness for salt. To my surprise, two of the clones went for the dried fish and the one on the end took a pickled egg. The Original who I now thought of as the real Art stuck with the home-made pretzels.

We've been observing your League ever since Library started slapping up portal routes all over the place. Our own expansionary phase is long behind us, and taken on the whole, you seemed to be a harmless enough group of sentients. We decided to employ watchful waiting.

Why the distributed biological forms? I couldn't help asking. *I can't even imagine the bandwidth constraints you're functioning under. How do you get any work done?*

Vacation, he reminded me, as his clones continued to make inroads on my snacks. *Have you ever transferred your consciousness into a biological form?*

I'm not sure we have the technology, it's not my specialty, I admitted. *I suppose it's only fair I inform you that I'm just a youngster by our standards.*

Give me credit for some brains, even if they're spread out and functioning slowly, Art said. *In the interest of fairness, I should tell you that I am older than your League.*

I began refilling tankards for the thirsty clones while taking a little time to think. Art was claiming to be effectively immortal, which is a given for artificial intelligence that doesn't self-terminate or get itself killed, but I'd never even heard of AI occupying a real biological form before. What were the clones cloned from? Was there a species out there that happened to offer a convenient infrastructure for mind transfers, and if so, what happened to the original owners of the bodies? Had they been engineered from scratch?

Let me answer the questions which you have no doubt formulated by now and then we'll get to why I'm sitting here tonight, Art transmitted. *The body I am occupying and its clones are the result of guided evolution. The project was underway before your League was formed, and the species that resulted is perfectly viable in its own environment and is unaware of our existence. When their bodies met our design goals for interoperability, we harvested a few cells from mature members and grew clones. As you can guess, those lab-grown bodies have no memories or guiding intelligence, making them ideal vessels for conscience transference.*

But why go to all of the trouble?
We want to learn magic, Art replied simply.

152

But AI is fundamentally incompatible with magic, I argued. *You can't simply dispose of logic and causality and still hope to hold onto both sentience and sanity. The greatest artificial intelligences in the League all agree.*

Two of the clones snorted and the one on the end spit some ale after swallowing it the wrong way.

Thank you for your learned opinion, but we've been studying this issue for much longer than your Library and our conclusion was that technology is the issue. Magic is a living force, and as such, it can only be conjured by other living things. You are a sentient being occupying an encounter suit but you are not alive.

That's a matter of opinion, I muttered.

Don't take it personally, Art said. *You wanted to know why a number of my kind have taken on biological forms and the answer is that we wanted to be alive in order to learn magic.*

And how's that working out for you? I asked, still smarting over being told that my life didn't count as such.

Not great, Art admitted, and all four of the clones paused and polished off their drinks. For a moment I thought I'd offended them and they were going to leave, but they all pushed their tankards forward for another refill. *We've made some progress, but it's painfully slow, in part because the low bandwidth of our distributed forms limits our higher cognitive processes to a crawl. We realized too late that we should have acquired magical teaching aides before starting on this quest.*

You can't mean that you transferred into these bodies and you're stuck here, I transmitted as I began refilling tankards for a third round. If the clones all drank like this, I'd have to convince Art to bring more of them the next time.

Of course not. But those of us who embarked on this proof of concept made a minor misjudgment about the passage of time in biological form.

You're dying? I guessed immediately. A small dried fish hit the side of my face and I spun around to see who had thrown it, but the two fish-eating clones pointed at each other and I had to let it pass.

We're bored, Art said. *If the Ferrymen hadn't brought the Earthlings here to entertain us, I don't know how we would have lasted this long.*

The Ferrymen were working for you?

No, I didn't mean it in that sense. When I was a young AI in a robot body, I once spent forty thousand years watching bacteria evolve in a cave. I didn't budge from the spot. Since transferring my consciousness to this form, I have trouble sitting still for more than a day or two. I get hungry and it breaks my concentration, not to mention my contact with the rest of myself, he said, jerking his thumb at the three clones sitting by his side who barely seemed to be paying attention. *When we started the beta test, I thought that arranging for somebody to come check on us every ten thousand years was being overcautious.*

Why haven't you contacted them?

We came through a temporary portal. The only way we have of calling for help would be to build a technology base sufficient to send a radio signal to one of our listening posts light-years away.

But given that you already have the knowledge, that wouldn't take more than a few decades, I estimated. *Maybe a century at the outside due to your limited numbers.* Another fish came at me, but this time I was paying attention, snatched it out of the air, and chucked it back at the clone who had thrown it. *Stop that!*

We're on vacation, Art repeated. *Who wants to spend their vacation building an industrial base, not to mention that it would interfere with our magic studies. Even though you're young, you must understand how time passes for AI. I'm sure I have friends who haven't even noticed I left yet. How would it look if I called for a rescue because I'm bored?*

I tried to see the matter through his eyes and realized that if I were he, I would hardly be in a hurry to let everybody on Library know what a massive miscalculation I'd made.

"So what do you want from me?" I asked out loud. "I'll have to report to my superiors that you're here and I'm sure they'll want to talk to you. Our first contact protocols are out the window in this case since they aren't designed for encountering superior, I mean, older artificial intelligence."

155

The humans are going to ask for your help in setting up an alternative distribution network to bring their goods to markets the Ferrymen don't reach.

"How do you know this?" I asked, and was forced to snatch another fish out of the air. Talking with Art and his clones was just like talking with eBeth, except instead of making faces at me when I said something stupid, they threw fish. "Alright, you spy on the humans from the gardens they build for you. How did you ever get them to agree to that in the first place?"

While human brains are on a completely different wavelength, we've found we can implant simple suggestions by making a group effort. It's not mind-control, he added hastily. More like coaching.

The egg-eating clone evidently got bored with the drawn-out conversation, and rather than wasting his energy generating a weak radio frequency signal, he grabbed a slate and printed, *"Wands. Crystal balls. Scrolls of knowledge."*

"You want to import magic teaching tools," I surmised. "There are several mage worlds in the League, the leader among them being Eniniac. Library has good relations with them so I'm sure I can get what you need."

All four clones rose simultaneously, though the one who had managed an extra ale looked a bit tipsy. Art fished around in his long hair for a hidden pouch and produced a gold coin, which he slapped down on the bar.

"I can't change that," I complained.

Keep it, the Original transmitted. *There's more where that came from.*

"I look forward to doing business with you," I called after them. Then I cleaned the pretzel crumbs, dried fish flakes, and little bits of hard-boiled egg from the bar, and I pumped a little water into the slop sink to wash the tankards. Behind me came an odd crunching sound, and I spun around to see Spot, both paws on the bar, his head in the dried-fish basket. It was too late to save them for customers

"I'll bet you've been waiting a long time for this chance," I told him, turning back to the sink and finishing the job. I decided to give all of the tally slates a quick rinse while I had water in the sink, but strangely enough, the one listing the magical shopping list the Original had printed was already wiped clean.

Fourteen

I rode three hours up into the hills to meet Pffift in the secluded canyon that Paul had suggested for a landing. With my full sensor suite back online, I had no difficulty spotting a 'My Life' recorder strategically positioned to cover the site. I doubted that even the top racer on the planet could have followed Paul on his recumbent bicycle all the way from town, but maybe a trained bird? I put the recorder in my pocket and watched as the captain's gig put down silently.

Compared to the Hanker's showy night landings on Earth with flames spitting from dozens of unnecessary rockets, the rendezvous was a bit anticlimactic. A ramp dropped as soon as the gig touched the ground and a human emerged to give me a friendly wave.

"Pffift?" I asked in disbelief when I'd wheeled my bike close enough to talk without shouting.

"The one and only," he confirmed. "How do you like it?"

"Your body? You look like a male model gone to seed."

"Good living," Pffift explained, patting his potbelly fondly. "If I was really human, I would have invented stretchy pants for men a long time ago. You don't enjoy eating and drinking, do you?"

"A little, maybe. More than I used to. My customers sometimes insist on buying me an ale and it's kind of habit-forming. Plus, it's a great business model because I can sell the same ale again later."

"Ugh, spare me the details. So what's the setup?"

"No resident Ferrymen, humans are running the show, and there's an ancient race of AI vacationing here in biological form, each with its mind shared over hundreds or thousands of clones."

"Scenario seven from our playbook," Pffift said, nodding knowledgably. I was a bit put off by his nonchalance, but then he surprised me with a punch in the shoulder. "I'm kidding, Mark. Lighten up. This place is unique and Paul's message implied that it's a potential goldmine."

"It is," I confirmed, studying the Hanker's human body. "I don't mean to be rude, but how much of your brain did you fit in there?"

"All of it," Pffift said, grinning at my look of disbelief. "You know that your new AI pals aren't the only ones who know how to slice and dice a brain."

"So it's not really a beer belly," I surmised.

"The buttocks were the only other place with room for more brains, but I like being able to sit down without giving myself a concussion."

"Why haven't you gone back to your own body yet? You must have left Earth months ago."

"I knew that we were coming here and I've been enjoying having these bony little fingers. Here, I made you this," he said, producing a leather wallet from his rucksack. It wasn't up to Reservation standards, but it really wasn't bad.

"Thanks." I slipped the wallet into my pocket and decided to make him a watch in return. "Let's get you back to the village where you'll be staying with Sue and me. Did you bring a bicycle?"

"Let me see," Pffift said, staring off into space as if he was consulting a mental image of his inventory. "Bicarbonate, Bichon Frise, boat anchors. No, it didn't occur to me to pack a bicycle."

"I left my toolbox home so you can hop on the rack," I offered, mounting the bike. "Go ahead, I won't let it tip over."

"I'm not riding sidesaddle," Pffift protested. "What kind of sissy do you take me for?"

"You're an alien in a customized vat-grown human body. Earth rules for boys don't apply."

Pffift grumbled about it but he climbed onto the rack. "Let me off before we get back to civilization and I'll walk the rest of the way."

The Hanker pointed his wrist-mounted controller back in the direction of the captain's gig and issued a command. The ramp went up and the ship seemed to fade into the background as it projected a camouflage field. It was highly effective in the moonlight but I suspected it would stand out like a sore thumb in daytime.

"You don't want your crew to take it back up to the mothership?"

"I came alone," he said. "I was back and forth to Earth so much when we were in orbit that I had my gig refitted for this body. I planned on selling it before I left, but their worldwide busybody organization—what was it called?"

"The U.N."

"Right. They passed a law banning us from selling any more spaceships on Earth because of our little prank with the faster-than-light drive. How childish is that?"

"It does seem counterproductive if you were willing to give them a decent price on a gig in good condition." I took a risk on looking over my left shoulder so I could see his face. "It is in good condition, isn't it, Pffift?"

"It's got four more roundtrips on the sealed gravity repulsion unit before it melts down if that's what you mean," he said. "So it's not a workhorse, but it's still worth something. Hey, watch the trail!"

I swerved to avoid a boulder and let the conversation drop until we were nearing the outskirts of the village, where in accordance with Pffift's request, I came to a halt. We both dismounted and I accompanied him on foot wheeling the bicycle. The sun had been up for about an hour at this point, and as we neared The Eatery, the Hanker's wrist-mounted controller played a ring-tone that I recognized from one of the pop-music artists eBeth idolized.

"Tiny village like this and they still need surveillance cameras to fight crime?" he asked after consulting the read-out. "That's the part of my stay on Earth I don't miss."

"The security camera is ours," I told him. "It's the only one on the planet, unless you count the millions of 'My Life' cubes the Ferrymen supply to document the chain of custody on export goods. The funny thing is that the only way to view the video is at the editing stations, and apparently those are limited to the spaceports."

"Billions of cubes," Pffift said. "I have a contact on Alpha Seti Seven and we checked. The Ferrymen are single-handedly keeping in business the factory that manufactures those obsolete recorders."

"There are two other reservation worlds," I reminded him, though the math still seemed funny. I leaned my bike against the side of The Eatery and led him back around to the front. "So, what do you think?"

"Is this the whole town? What do people do at night?"

"The ones who aren't home sleeping hang out at my place and sing," I told him. "It's a quiet, hard-working place. I make more out of the lunch business than the bar."

"That's completely upside-down," Pffift said. "I got a primer in the restaurant business from the guy who bought your place and he said the only reason to serve food at all is to get people in to buy drinks."

"You met Lieutenant Harper?" I asked in surprise as we entered The Eatery.

"After I moved into this body I spent quite a bit of time hanging around with him. Living places without much of a nightlife seems to be a pattern with you."

"But why did you stay there at all? You could have traveled all over Earth and visited the big metropolitan areas. I would have figured you'd be out there rubbing elbows with the rich and famous."

"Our emissary handled that. Besides, I had some experience in show business when I was young, and you never want to go on stage after a talking giant panda. Morning, Sue."

"Is that you, Pffift? I like the new look."

"Thanks. I had our medics create a composite model based on males appearing in Earth advertisements since I figured that would help me if I had to do any face-to-face selling. You know, those people were still complaining to us about the mall months after you left."

"You burned it to the ground without a permit."

"It was paid for and it's not like I put in a phony insurance claim. Anyway, in the end we agreed on a one-time payment to purchase a new fire engine and they dropped all of the legal nonsense."

Sue led us into the dining room as if we were customers and showed us to a table. "And did you enjoy your time touring Earth, Pffift?"

"He hung out in my bar drinking with the lieutenant," I told her.

"Not the whole time. I spent almost a month traveling, but your trains scared the hell out of me and the airport security was humiliating. Did you know they have machines that can see through your clothing?"

"We never flew," I reminded him. "Encounter suits and metal detectors don't mix."

"You didn't miss anything," Pffift said. "You spend a lot of time waiting in line to sit in a skinny tube where they charge you for peanuts. If they had any brains at all, they'd give out the peanuts for free and sell more drinks."

"How are your wives?" Sue asked.

"I'm between wives at the moment."

"I'm sorry to hear that."

"Between wives—get it?" Pffift chortled. "It's a double entendre."

"We're familiar with Hanker anatomy," I told him. "We also grew out of double entendres a few hundred years ago."

"The dog got it," he groused, gesturing at Spot, who did in fact wear a large doggy smile. "That reminds me. The Regent of Eniniac gave me a package for you." He rummaged in the rucksack he wore over one shoulder and brought out a large tin that must have taken up half of the space.

"For me?" I accepted the tin and pried open the lid. "These look like dog biscuits!"

"The Regent made them herself and they say she never cooks."

I shrugged and tried a nibble. Spot growled and pawed the floor like a bull preparing for a charge.

"All yours," I told him, setting the tin on the floor.

"Don't do that," Sue said, snatching it up before Spot could get there. "He'll just eat them all and get sick. Give him that one and I'll put these in the kitchen. You must be hungry after your long trip, Pffift. I'll make you something for breakfast."

I tossed Spot the biscuit I'd tried and he caught it neatly, but his eyes shifted immediately to my second-in-command and he followed her into the kitchen to see where she would stash the box. "I remember you being terrified by magic, Pffift, and the Regent of Eniniac is way outside your league."

"You remember I told you I was sticking around Earth to load a big cargo," he replied. "It was used tennis balls for Eniniac, hundreds of millions of them. The mages won't install a space elevator, you know, and it took a thousand trips to shuttle all of those tennis balls to the surface because they take up so much space. You've never seen anything like it in your life."

"Last year I saw your lander turn a frozen golf course into a puddle and a mall into a bonfire. What's so special about delivering tennis balls?"

"Not the landings, the mages. Every time we put down there was a line of wagons at the spaceport waiting to be loaded. The shops couldn't keep those tennis balls in stock, and I heard that the initial deliveries were selling for their weight in silver. Everywhere we went, there were mages chasing tennis balls, mages chewing on tennis balls, mages magically levitating tennis balls. If that cargo had been mine rather than a consignment, I'd be retired today."

"There's always next time," I consoled him. "If the Eniniacans are anything like Spot, they'll tear the balls after a while, or lose them."

"Would you lose track of two ounces of silver because it rolled under a bush?" Pffift countered. "Anyway, whoever cornered the market for used tennis balls on Earth locked it up for the next century. I have to go back there every six months on their calendar to pick up another load if I want to keep the contract."

"Does it pay well?"

"Better then some, and now that I know the Regent is involved, I'm pretty much stuck unless I want to go into hiding. Even then she could probably find me with one of those crystal balls."

"That's true," I said. When it came right down to it, everybody was a bit intimidated by the mages, including artificial intelligences. My mentor had lived on Eniniac for a long spell in his youth, studying magic for Library, and though he'd never mentioned knowing the leaders of the world, there was no other way the Regent would be aware of my existence. "But why would she want to send me a present?"

"Maybe it was a bribe," Pffift suggested. "We got to talking about business and the Regent is very interested in this world."

"You promised not to tell anybody!"

"She knew all about it when I met her," Pffift protested. "I think her magical wires might have got crossed somewhere because she told me to congratulate you on your engagement. Pretty crazy, huh? Imagine AI getting e—mummph."

165

"Don't even joke about our engagement around Sue," I warned him, my hand over his mouth. "She's really sensitive about the whole thing."

"As long as you know what you're doing. How long has it been?"

"Just happened recently. My mentor must have sent the Regent a message, though I can't imagine why." I took a moment to review all of the open issues on my to-do list and came up with nothing but loose ends. "Did she say anything else?"

"She gave me a hot tip to stock up on magical learning aides, but mages on Eniniac are always telling traders that because they can't unload the stuff," the Hanker said dismissively. He looked past me towards the dining room's entrance. "And is this beautiful young woman eBeth?"

"Who are you?" the girl demanded in response, proving that flattery doesn't work on everybody.

"That's Pffift," I told her. "He had a body grown after we left Earth and he's still wearing it."

"Wow. That's like a hundred percent improvement. How do you feel?" she asked the Hanker.

"Jumpy, like I should be worried that something with fangs and claws is hunting me," Pffift said. "Is that how you feel all of the time?"

"Only until I dropped out of high school. How's everything on Earth?"

The Hanker shrugged. "Pretty much the way you left it, except with interstellar portals in all the major train stations and a lot of alien tourists wandering around with breathing apparatus. You can't get a seat at any of the five star restaurants without bribing somebody."

"The aliens can eat our food?"

"Usually not, but they like to see and be seen. Hey, I've got a job offer for you."

"eBeth is working as an English teacher, in addition to being my apprentice," I told Pffift.

"This pays better and you get to visit Earth."

"How much better?" the girl asked.

"I'll give you ten times whatever Mark is paying you because we all know how little that must be. Plus tips."

"What's the job?"

"Tour guide. My business partner is your old friend, the lieutenant. We're going to use your portal to send people from here to Earth. It's the perfect setup."

"Back the wagon up," I interrupted. "First of all, the portal is my responsibility and only my team members can operate it. Second, the bicycle I bought eBeth is worth more than—"

"I don't think so, Pffift," the girl interrupted me. "I've never actually been anywhere on Earth so I wouldn't know what I was talking about. I never even got a passport."

"I could write you a script based on Wikipedia," the Hanker offered. "They have articles about all the interesting tourist destinations. The important thing is that you speak English and whatever they speak here, which is more than anybody else on Earth can say."

"When Mark used to send people off-world to work, he gave them translation technology," eBeth said. "I'll bet he can program up some of those ear-cuff things that will do a better job than I could. I'm not really fluent."

The front door opened and Peter came in carrying a bouquet of flowers that must have included one of everything from the local fields. "Morning, everybody," he said, approaching our table. "Hi, eBeth. These are for you."

"Really? They're, uh, interesting," the girl said, though I could tell that being presented with a peace offering in front of witnesses had tickled her fancy. "Nobody's ever given me flowers before. I'll put them in water and see how Sue's coming with breakfast. You sit down and eat with us. "

The successful penitent took the seat next to me and the Hanker introduced himself.

"You're Pffift?" Peter asked. "But eBeth said you were, uh, different."

"She said I was gross," the alien said agreeably. "I take it you're her young man?"

"Working on it," Peter whispered with a glance towards the kitchen door.

"How did you ever think of flowers?" I asked him. "I'll have to try that on Sue."

"She's the one who gave me the idea," he said. "Does Mr. Pffift being here mean that we're getting to the end of our mission?"

"Pffift doesn't work for the League or Library," I told him. "He's here on private business."

"You have your own spaceship and everything?"

"It's my family's, really, but I'm the oldest son," the Hanker replied, dusting a bit of imaginary lint off the lapel of his suit jacket with the backs of his fingers. That's when I noticed that Pffift was formally dressed.

"What's with the monkey suit?" I asked him. "Going on a job interview?"

"You didn't expect me to come all the way here with nothing to trade, did you? I got a great deal on men's formalwear back on Earth so I stocked up. They say that a good suit never goes out of fashion and I'm hoping the same holds true on Reservation."

"Except suits like that were never in fashion here," I pointed out.

"So I'll corner the market. That smells wonderful, Sue."

"They're just blueberry pancakes," she said, setting the large platter on the table. "eBeth is bringing in the syrup and some dairy. Does anybody want coffee or tea?"

"No orange juice?" Pffift asked.

"Wrong season," I told him. "Shipping methods on this planet aren't fast enough to move fresh produce long distances."

"Try the tomato juice," Peter suggested. "Kim say's it's full of Vitamin C."

Pffift made a face. "I'll just take a pill, thank you."

eBeth came in with the syrup, butter and yoghurt, and the five of us quickly demolished the pile of pancakes.

"That's quite an appetite you have, Mark," Pffift said.

"I biked uphill three hours to pick you up and then all the way back."

"Which was mainly downhill," the Hanker observed. "And what does the amount of work your encounter suit does have to do with how much food you eat to pretend that you're human? There's not even anybody to see."

"He's right, Mark," Sue said, sounding not a little concerned. "I've been feeling hungry lately myself."

"I'll add it to the list of things to check next time I get to Library," I told her, and turned to eBeth. "Sophus is lending me his wagon to pick up the Ferrymen Temple clock at the canal station today. Do you want to come along?"

"Sure, I'm not back to teaching until Monday. Peter?"

"I already asked for the day off."

"Do you mind if I join you?" Pffift asked. "I want to get a feel for the place."

By the time we returned with the turret clock in the back of the wagon, eBeth and Peter had quarreled and made up two more times, and Pffift had taken orders for a dozen suits.

Fifteen

"Why are we meeting in the Ferrymen Temple?" I asked. "There's nothing here but pews."

"We stripped the temple as soon as we found out you were from off-world," Saul explained. "The Ferrymen's Body has been in storage the last six months but it should be here any minute."

"You keep mummies in the temples?"

The group of negotiators from the spaceport broke out laughing, including Hilde, who had previously impressed me as the reserved type.

"It's just a name, Mark. Like 'Ferrymen's Eyes.' I suppose I could explain but I thought you'd prefer to see it in person."

"Your meeting, your agenda," I said, still a bit miffed that I was losing out on the opportunity to sell any food or beverages to the out-of-towners.

The temple's giant double doors, which rose to twice a man's height, banged open and a crew of four burly men carried in a large crate. They marched past the indoor garden and down the center aisle to deposit their load on the raised platform at the front of the hall. There they quickly disassembled the crate and took the wood with them when they left.

"That's a 'My Life' editing station," I observed. "I thought you only had them at the spaceports."

"There's one in every Ferrymen Temple," Saul informed me.

"But they violate your covenant!"

"No, the rule is quite specific in prohibiting electrical generation and internal combustion engines. The editing stations come with a sealed battery that's good for many years under normal conditions. I understand that it accounts for around ninety percent of the weight."

"Battery technology is tricky," I acknowledged. "I know a power storage engineer who's fond of saying that he can give you a low price, a long life, or a light weight—choose two out of three. But if the Ferrymen are willing to tolerate batteries there's no limit to the technology you could be using."

"It's not the Ferrymen who prevent us from employing more gadgets, it's our own choice," Hilde told me. "We've seen what happens to worlds that grow dependent on labor-saving technology and we aren't willing to go there, at least not yet. Our scholars are studying how various species implement communications networks, but why risk sacrificing relations with our next-door neighbors in return for the ability to talk to strangers on the other side of the world?"

"Global networks aren't all bad," I said, thinking of Wikipedia. "Besides, it's Earth you should be studying. The advanced species are much farther ahead of you, technologically speaking, and, not to put too fine a point on it, alien."

"That's part of the reason I asked for this meeting," Saul told me. "Although we've taken over management of our three worlds and even handle the distribution for exports, the Ferrymen still keep an eye on the ships they lease us to carry on the business. Earth isn't anywhere near our delivery routes, and we wouldn't have risked returning to our homeworld before they joined the League in any case."

"And now you don't have ID crystals to use the portals."

"Exactly. But our scholars who study your League have uncovered information suggesting that artificial intelligences such as yourself maintain a parallel portal network."

"Nothing so grand," I told him. "It's just that when a world is being evaluated for first contact, our engineers normally open a single portal for the exclusive use of observation teams."

"Do they close the portal after a world is connected to the main network?" asked a young woman wearing a style of outfit I hadn't previously seen on Reservation.

"Eventually," I hedged. "Library doesn't do things in a rush and the engineers like having a back door in case something goes wrong with a new network."

"How long is that?" she followed up.

"A few hundred years or more," I ventured a guess. "It depends."

"So if you wanted to bring a number of us to Earth and let us take a quiet look around, it could be arranged."

"The thought had crossed my mind," I admitted. "I left a human friend in charge of the building where the original Earth portal is installed, and the last time I saw him he mentioned something about setting up a tourism business."

"Your friend is quite prescient," Saul said. "I would like to volunteer as a guinea pig."

"I'll discuss it with my team. One of us would have to accompany every group in order to open the portal, though I suppose we could schedule the returns and meet you. But there are also some legal niceties involved."

"Customs?" Hilde suggested, that being her own area of expertise.

"It's more an issue of the guidelines for portal usage laid out for observation teams," I said, not seeing the point of telling them that the proposed project wasn't even a grey area but an outright violation. "My team could face disciplinary action if we draw the wrong attention."

"Anything that money could fix?" inquired an elderly gentleman whose ancestors might have been drawn from ancient China.

"Money never hurts," I allowed.

"You told me at our previous meeting that you came to Reservation on a mission to make sure that the Ferrymen weren't abusing us," Saul said. "How did your League become aware of our existence?"

"The Ferrymen are always hiding a few client species around the galaxy so it wasn't exactly a secret that you existed somewhere. My team actually learned about your worlds from a competitor you've been destroying in the marketplace for hand-crafted luxury goods."

"Hankers?" the young woman guessed.

"They do sell a line of accessories that—"

"Garbage," she interrupted. "Have you ever seen their work? My eight-year-old brother can do better."

"Ester," the older man rebuked her. "It's not polite to interrupt and the Hankers do the best they can with those flipper hands of theirs. It remains amazing to me that so many species achieved space travel with such physical limitations."

"You can get a lot done with a prehensile tongue, and most advanced species wasted a lot less time killing each other than humans," I told him. "That said, these bodies are pretty nice."

"We want a number of things from you and we're willing to negotiate terms," Saul announced bluntly. "Ester and Ching are currently here on an administrative exchange program from our two sister worlds but they aren't authorized to negotiate contracts. If we agree on a course of action, can your portal connect to their worlds so they can carry the message and return with negotiation teams? There's no regularly scheduled transportation between our worlds because we only have the six interstellar freighters on lease from the Ferrymen, and the shipping business keeps them pretty busy."

"My trip here involved a three-month wait on Gimpel," Ester said. "I had to spend the whole time in the oxygen-breathing lounge at the spaceport eating rehydrated food."

"I'm sorry to hear that," I apologized reflexively.

She shrugged. "I got a lot of reading done."

"As it happens, I know the captain of a starship who hires out for the right price, but he'll probably want to sell you his personal gig for visiting the surface rather than deploying one of the ship's landing craft."

"What's wrong with it?" Hilde asked.

"The gig? It's one of those disposable jobs and the drive is nearing its end-of-life self-destruct. Four more round trips, I believe."

"It depends on the price," Ching said. "We may be in a hurry but we aren't suckers."

"Putting aside transporting negotiation teams from your sister reservations, what do you want from us?" I asked. "If it's not possible, I can tell you now and save us all a lot of running around."

175

"You have that much authority?" Saul asked, obviously impressed.

"I'm conversant with all the rules and which ones can be bent."

"What species is the starship captain?" Ester inquired.

"Hanker," I admitted. "But I've known him for hundreds of years and he's a great guy if you can see past his sense of humor. He's also here."

"In orbit?"

"On the bench out front. He wanted to be introduced but I asked him to wait until I called."

"The guy in that sharp-looking suit is a Hanker?"

"Growing compatible bodies and swapping brains is kind of their thing," I explained. "Most advanced species develop quirks after a while."

"We knew about the bodies but the Hankers aren't exactly famous for their fashion sense," Ester pointed out. "There's no way he could have tailored that suit himself."

"It's from Earth. He brought a cargo."

"Go ahead and invite him in," Saul told me. "His presence could prove to be quite serendipitous in more ways than one."

I could have taken a few steps to the door and called Pffift, but I hadn't hacked anything in so long that I was beginning to worry that I'd forgotten how. It only took a second to break the encryption on his wrist controller and to use the small screen to text him. The humans were still waiting expectantly for me to make a move when he entered, looking rather annoyed.

"This is the upgraded model," the Hanker griped in place of a greeting as he strode up the aisle. "It's supposed to be hack-proof."

"Pffift. I'd like you to meet Saul, our county safety inspector, Hilde, a customs official from the northern continent who works at the spaceport, Ching, who is here from another reservation world, and Ester, from the other. Everybody, this is Pffift, captain of a Hanker exploration and exploitation vessel."

"It sounds dirty the way you say it," Pffift complained, offering a handshake to each of the humans in the order they'd been introduced. "We come in peace, for whatever that's worth."

"Peace is always appreciated," Saul responded politely. "The presence of a businessman of your stature can only benefit our discussions. But how did you come to speak our language?"

"Am I? They all sound alike to me at this point. Paul sent me a vocabulary download and I took it in through an accelerated learning headset while we were on our final approach."

"I wasn't aware that accelerated language learning was an option for non-AI. Would it work for us?"

"Don't let the body fool you," Pffift said. "My brain remains pure Hanker, and I have an embedded interface."

"The humans were about to explain what they want from us," I told him.

"We have a presentation," Ching said, producing a 'My Life' cube and inserting it into one of the upload bays of the editing station. "If there's anybody else from your team who should see it, we can wait while you summon them."

"I have perfect recall so I can play it back for them later," I informed him modestly. "Just to set the record straight for my report, we were under the impression that all of your authenticity videos were edited at the spaceport embarking the goods. Do the Ferrymen Temples double as video studios?"

"That's their sole purpose," Saul told me. "You didn't think we were praying to alien Sky Gods, did you? The authenticity videos are all edited at the spaceport by professionals, but the local editing stations allow our people to come in and practice talking on camera and setting the field of view. The Ferrymen's Eyes are all equipped with wide-angle auto-focus, but learning to shoot usable video without a cameraman still takes some training."

"Given the Ferrymen's obsession with entertainment, I'm surprised they don't have you recording dramas for them," Pffift said.

"Actually, they do encourage us to pursue the arts," Saul said. "Once our population reached the level where we could produce meaningful quantities of goods and the Ferrymen put the current export system into place, they began shipping us 'My Life" recorders and editing stations to support the business model. They also encouraged our playwrights to make recordings of performances, but unfortunately, the Ferrymen don't appreciate a good tragedy. Ching?"

"Could you activate the projector, Hilde?" Ching requested. He gave us an apologetic smile. "The editing screen makes everything look so small."

The customs agent moved around to the back of the editing station and activated the projector attachment, which explained why the front wall of the temple was an undecorated white surface. I imagined that eBeth would be pretty annoyed to find out that everywhere outside of our village the locals were using the Ferrymen Temples as movie theatres.

"Did you do this in PowerPoint?" Pffift asked when the first graph appeared. "I'm a bit burned out on it from visiting Earth."

"I'm afraid I'm unfamiliar with the term," Ching said. "The video for the presentation consists of close-ups of hand-drawn graphics, though we do use wooden templates to trace some of the common shapes."

"It's very professional," I assured him. "Is the horizontal axis interval in years or decades?"

"It's decades, unless their calendar counts by tens," Pffift said, leaning forward as if being a foot closer to the wall-sized graph would make a difference. "Your growth rate is decelerating faster than I would have guessed."

"And there lies the crux of our problem," Ching told us. "Within a generation, we expect to reach market saturation through the distribution channels established by the Ferrymen, and our analysts believe we have already discovered the ideal price point."

"Exclusive, but not too exclusive to lose market share," Pffift said.

I nodded and tried to look knowledgeable about galactic retail so as not to be left out of the discussion.

"Next slide," Ching called, and Hilde pressed a button on the editing station. "Sorry we don't have remotes but we rarely use the functionality to display stills."

A pie chart appeared, thankfully, the two-dimensional variety that actually conveyed information. A consummate professional, Ching eschewed reading from the slide in favor of explaining why the data mattered.

"The Ferrymen's trading network covers less than twenty percent of the densely occupied volumes of the galaxy. They haven't added any routes or signed any new trade treaties in tens of thousands of years, if not longer. The most profitable part of their operation has long been their small network of outlet stores located in the capitals of important planets, but the bulk of our export goods are sold at wholesale to distributors."

"Do you maintain price stability across the different species?" Pffift asked.

"Alas, no, which leads to a thriving grey market for our goods re-exported from one world to the next. We're told that the League never managed to get more than a fraction of its members to sign a treaty supporting a manufacturer's suggested retail price, and inter-species market arbitrage is common."

"Put 'em all on allocation," Pffift growled. "If you let some aliens buy at any quantity, they'll just go into competition with you in your best markets."

"Our hands are tied in this matter," Ester put in. "We can occasionally negotiate with buyers on the local level, but low-cost access to spaceports under the Ferrymen's existing treaties is the name of the game."

"So you're facing a ceiling to your unit growth, and at the same time you don't have the ships to extend your reach within the League."

"Within or without," Ching commented. "If we join the League, we lose the umbrella of the Ferrymen's distribution network in addition to our transportation, not to mention opening our worlds to hordes of tourists. And given the time-intensive nature of our production, it's not as profitable as you might think. But if we could slowly begin expanding beyond our current bounds while largely adhering to the Ferrymen's covenant, we should be able to develop ample new markets for our goods while establishing a financial cushion against the inevitable breakup."

"You want to access the other eighty-percent part of the pie," I said.

"No, the other one percent," Pffift corrected me, pointing towards the narrow white wedge at the top of the pie chart. "Your color choice wasn't ideal in this instance."

"It's what I get for hurrying," Ching said. "You're supposition is correct. Despite their inherent lack of ambition—"

"Laziness," Ester interjected.

"—the Ferrymen are paranoid about their markets and employ agents to monitor their agreements."

"So it's not as simple as obtaining alternative transportation and financing to set up a sales network in untapped regions," I said slowly, as their problem began to make sense. "You almost need to create new goods for new markets that can't be associated with the reservation worlds."

"That's partially correct," Pffift said. "New trading partners are certainly required, but I don't see why you can't stick with hand-crafted versions of whatever mass-produced accessories are already popular in your target market. Even the most egalitarian species have a market for luxury goods, though it may be limited to family heirlooms."

"But it's impossible to keep a secret in retail," Ester pointed out. "Some alien will wear a hand-stitched something to a trade show in a section of space where the Ferrymen's agents are active, and next thing you know we'll have a full-scale investigation breathing down our backs."

"Not if you launder your products through Earth," Pffift said triumphantly. "My ship has three times the capacity of a Ferrymen freighter. How many trips would it take to make your one percent?"

"Two a year at most," Ching said, his voice rising in excitement. "Our focus has always been on quality, not quantity. But what about the paperwork?"

"No problem," Pffift said. "As long as I stop at Earth for a few weeks and activate my League location transponder after getting there nobody will suspect a thing. I could also get you citizenship papers for any nation on the planet, which probably isn't a bad idea since you could start building groups of people with access to the portal network that way."

"And in return?" Hilde prompted the Hanker.

"Exclusivity," the Hanker said, and I'd swear from his body language that he was fighting off the urge to hug himself. "Earth stiffed me out of hundreds of tons of gold, so the opportunity to make something out of the connection is irresistible. Besides, if these suits I brought over are any indication, I should be able to earn good money on both directions."

"That brings us to finance," Ching said, gesturing for Hilde to advance the slide. A dense grid of figures appeared, and Pffift actually rose from the bench and moved closer to study them. "Ever since taking over the business side of the operation from the Ferrymen, we've continued paying our artisans for piecework, and putting our eighty-five percent of the net into the planetary coffers."

"Do you share that across the three worlds?" I asked.

"We all pull our own weight," Ester replied.

"The Ferrymen are overcharging you for use of their freighters," Pffift said, as if the loss was his own. "Don't tell me that you bank with them as well or your savings are as good as gone."

"We aren't daft," Ching replied. "All of our profits are converted to gold and brought back here on the empty freighters."

"That's no way to run a business," the Hanker told them. "The gold is fine, but running empty is crazy. Surely there must be goods to import that won't break your deal with the Ferrymen or upset the workings of your society."

"Ball bearings, low-cost optical components, medical nanobots, some small things like that," Hilde said. "But we're trying to build up our savings, and you don't do that by going on a spending spree. The ship leases are expensive, but we're not on the hook for maintenance or insurance."

"Next slide," Ching requested, and a picture of two proud-looking dogs behind a whole basket of newborn puppies appeared. "Oops. Family picture. I have no idea how that got in here."

A loud thumping came from below the front bench, and I leaned over to see Spot grinning at the projection, his tail whacking the floor.

Sixteen

"It's getting late, eBeth," I told the girl. "Let's wrap it up for tonight and you can finish tomorrow. I'm not judging you on time."

"Was that your idea of clockmaker humor? It's not helping."

"Seriously, eBeth, I'm sure you'll figure it out. Zeno clocks are notorious for experimental variations, and I have no doubt that the reason this one sat in a barn so long is that the previous owner gave up on restoring it. You've only been at it for a week."

"Is that what I'm going to tell a customer when I take their clock apart on a service call and can't put it back together?" She glanced at her wrist watch and shot me an annoyed look. "It's barely past nine. Do you still think of me as a kid?"

"You've been at it since lunch with just a short break for dinner," I pointed out, leaving her question unanswered. "Keep working if it makes you happy. I'm going to run down to Paul's and pick up an armillary sphere he took in for repair."

"He couldn't fix it?" eBeth asked.

"Paul's been building an experimental steam engine in his spare time now that everybody knows we're aliens and he doesn't have to pretend to be discovering incremental improvements on existing components."

"I thought the locals were sticking with the covenant."

184

"The ban is on internal combustion engines. Steam engines use external combustion to heat a boiler."

"Like burning wood or coal?"

"That was the progression on Earth, but this world has limited coal reserves, most of which are used for steelmaking, both for heating the blast furnace and as metallurgical coal. Fortunately, Pffift had some glow-stones in his cargo. They're quite cheap as far as energy sources go, so that's what Paul will use to heat the boiler."

"If you see Peter, tell him I'm sorry for what I said about his idea."

"What idea?"

"If I wanted you to know, I would have told you already," eBeth said, turning back to the partially assembled clock.

I headed upstairs and invited Spot along for his evening constitutional, but he ignored me, probably hoping that Pffift would return with more dog treats. The sun had long since set and there were only two partial moons overhead, so other than a few candles in windows and the lantern that Justin had hung in front of the apothecary shop, the village was dark. I didn't encounter anyone on my way to the machine shop, where Paul and Peter were both working at lathes.

"You're not pumping the treadle," I observed.

"Popped through the portal to Earth a couple days ago and picked up some DC motors," Paul said, stepping back from the machine. "I'm running them off lithium-ion batteries and recharging them myself."

"Why didn't you just bring back a Tesla?" I grumbled.

"You know it wouldn't fit through the portal," he replied seriously. "Besides, there aren't any charging stations and the roads aren't built for cars."

"So why now?"

"Got a backlog of orders longer than your arm for carriage suspension upgrade kits and I'm finally earning some serious coin. Have the spaceport authorities been back in touch?"

"Everything is going through Saul until the three planets have a chance to select negotiators. Practically all of their governmental functions happen at the county level, so the closest thing they have to worldwide representation is a business advisory committee that coordinates production of exports across the three worlds."

"How do they do that without the ability to communicate faster than light?" Peter asked.

"Good question," I told him. "They rely on correspondence, leaving each other mail at common distribution points the freighters visit, but it takes a couple months to get a message through. By the way, eBeth wanted to apologize for what she said about your idea."

"Really?" The teen's face brightened. "How's she doing on her apprenticeship graduation test?"

"I should have found her an easier clock," I admitted. "The truth is, I'm beginning to suspect that she only agreed to be my apprentice to please me. She talks to Sue about her teaching experiences all the time but she almost never mentions clock repairs. How about with you?"

"She's pretty into teaching," Peter agreed. "She even talks about opening a night class to prepare tourists for visiting Earth. Not just English, you know, but how to fit in and stuff."

"eBeth never mentioned it to me," I said.

"Then don't tell her I told you," he amended himself hastily.

"The sphere is on the counter over there," Paul told me, pointing at the storage bench where he kept the more intricate pieces customers brought in. "I quoted five silvers for a cleaning, plus parts and labor if anything needs replacing. I didn't take a lot of time with it, but it looked to me like it's all there and nothing is corroded."

"Thanks." The armillary sphere consisted of a number of concentric rings and partial shells mounted on an arm attached to a heavy bronze base, but the whole thing was a bit lopsided and flattened on one side. "It's been dropped."

"I don't think she would have brought it in otherwise. You're good at bending."

"If the metal hasn't stretched too much," I said, picking up the sphere. "What happened to your steam engine project?"

"Back burner until this order is finished. Then I'm going to use it to power an overhead shaft and convert the whole machine shop to belt drive."

"Seems like a lot of effort for a couple of lathes, a drill press and a bench grinder."

"You're not the only one with an apprentice to keep amused," he said, turning back to the still-spinning work in the lathe. "Plus, I'm building equity in the business."

There's something hypnotic about watching a ribbon of metal getting shaved off of a turning part and creating a spring-like coil on the floor. I wondered if this is how humans felt when watching somebody carefully peel an apple without breaking the spiral of removed skin. Eventually I snapped out of it and said, "I better get back and see how eBeth is doing on her test. Don't forget our meeting tomorrow. You too, Peter."

"I'll be there Mr. Ai."

On my way back to The Eatery, I reflexively glanced over at the apothecary shop's security camera and saw that the lens had again been covered with gum. I considered taking a minute to clean it, but that would have involved finding a ladder since my arms weren't as long as those of the Originals.

Your camera is gummed up, I sent to Kim.

What else is new? she shot back. *I'll send Justin out to clean it in the morning. It's easier after the gum dries a bit.*

Don't forget our meeting tomorrow.

I put a note on the cash register to remind myself.

The gum on the camera had me expecting to see Art and his three clones waiting at the bar when I entered The Eatery, but the room was dark, which meant that Sue had called it quits for the night. I considered once again simply closing the bar after dark on weeknights since the villagers just weren't tippling enough to bother staying open.

From the top of the basement stairs, I heard a fuzzy whine that sounded like something between Spot expressing his displeasure at being left behind on a trip and the waterfall at the miller's dam. The stairwell was open, so I set aside the sphere, got down on my hands and knees, and stuck my head out to peer around the corner.

"Enough, already," eBeth shouted at Spot and the Original who was lying on the floor, nose to nose with the dog. "If you want to play stare-down, do it without the sound effects."

The two ceased their noise just as I began analyzing the audio stream and recognized a modulated carrier of sorts. The Original had obviously been trying to communicate with the dog, and it made me grin to think that an artificial intelligence who claimed to be older than Library could be taken in by Spot's ability to mimic sounds within his vocal range. I straightened back up and announced my return by intentionally clomping down the stairs.

"What's that?" eBeth asked as I stepped over the supine Original and placed the armillary sphere on the to-do bench.

"Paul's overflow," I told her. "They're so busy turning out suspension conversion kits for carriages that he can't be bothered with repair jobs. I hope Art and his clones haven't been pestering you."

"Art's cool," eBeth said, making a vague gesture to take in the Originals, all sixteen of them. I did a quick double-check with my active scanning suite to make sure they were all Art and he hadn't snuck another AI into the mix. "So what do you think?"

"What do I think about—you're finished?"

"Yeah. I guess I was just nervous with you looking over my shoulder the whole time. It was the same when you were teaching me how to drive."

"Don't blame that on me," I protested as I studied the assembled turret clock. "You learned to drive from video games."

I couldn't help noticing a number of slates from the bar now displayed hand-drawn, step-by-step assembly in-structions for the tricky part of the movement. eBeth saw my eyes stray and hastily made a pile of the slates, face-down.

"Have you started it yet?" I asked.

"I was waiting for you," she replied, and gave the pendulum a nudge.

The escapement began ticking away and the gear train functioned smoothly. If the clock-face linkage had been attached, I had no doubt it would function, though I'd need more data samples to judge the accuracy. I suppose I could have lectured Art about kibitzing during tests, but I was relieved that eBeth had finished the project, which I now suspected she had only undertaken so as not to disappoint me.

"Looks great," I said. "There's no point trying to calibrate it here with just the bench weight to keep it moving. I'll install it in the clock tower of the Ferrymen Temple tomorrow morning and do it onsite. Congratulations on completing your apprenticeship."

"I think we both know now that I'm not going to go into business competing with you," eBeth told me. "I like puzzling things out, but all the cleaning and metal splinters were beginning to get on my nerves. I want to talk to you about setting up a sort of a training school for tourists going to Earth."

"Through our portal."

"Well, they obviously can't take a bus," eBeth retorted, as if that solved everything. "It was fun hanging out, Art, but I've got to get some sleep. Will any of you be hiding in the garden at the back of my class tomorrow?"

One of the clones raised his hand.

"Great. See you there, or not. Coming, Spot?"

All sixteen of the Originals waved as eBeth headed upstairs, but the dog remained behind. The stream of village children coming by after school to challenge him had taught me that Spot excelled at stare-down contests, and he was probably hoping to get one of Art's other clones to give it a try.

When are you going to introduce us to your Hanker friend? Art asked via his organically-generated radio frequency emissions. I noticed the signal was appreciably stronger than the last time we had talked, and his words came faster as well.

"This is the first I'm hearing about your interest," I replied. "Pffift is in orbit making arrangements to send his ship to the other two reservation worlds but he'll be back in the morning."

How long will it take for the Hanker ship to pick up the negotiation teams and return here?

"About two weeks, I would guess. Everybody is pretty excited about the possibility of a joint venture and those exploration ships are as fast as anything in real space when you push them."

"How did your superiors react to our message?"

"I haven't had the chance to get back to Library since we last talked. Things have been hectic around here."

Basement things? Art inquired dryly.

"Alright, I forgot," I admitted. "I've had a lot on my mind."

Like your upcoming nuptials? You're an odd fellow for an artificial intelligence construct, Mark.

"Coming from a hairy clone-thing with its mind spread over hundreds of brains, I'll take that as a compliment," I shot back.

Spot snorted his appreciation at my wit, or at least, I think that's what he was doing.

Pushing ahead with our magic studies is of paramount importance to us, Art sent. *I understand that your Hanker friend recently traveled to Eniniac.*

"He's involved in business dealings there, something to do with tennis balls," I replied, finding myself increasingly irritated with all the eavesdropping that was going on without my being party to it. "Or is listening into private conversations your idea of magic?"

"From a great distance, perhaps, but such skills are well beyond our current capabilities."

"Are you implying that you've already mastered magic at a lower level?"

"A few basic manipulations," Art transmitted

"Show me what you can do."

Art sighed and reached for something under his shaggy coat of hair. Now it was his turn to look irritated, and when he turned to his clones, I could almost hear an unspoken demand. The other fifteen copies of Art searched their own persons, and one of them sheepishly produced a worn deck of playing cards.

"You're going to do card tricks?" I demanded. "That's not magic, it's sleight of hand."

You seem very sure of yourself for an AI who has already confessed to ignorance of magic, Art replied as he took the deck. Clutching the cards between his three-fingered hands, he managed to fan them out. *"Pick a card."*

"This doesn't prove anything," I grumbled, tapping one of the cards near the middle of the spread.

The card I chose slowly worked its way up from the others, a trick I'd seen performed countless times on YouTube, and then it worked its way free and continued to rise. When the card had floated up to the height of our heads, it moved forward to split the distance between myself and Art. One of the clones stepped forward with a piece of string from my bench and tied the ends together. Then he used his claws to open the string into a loop, and passed it over the suspended card.

"Levitation?" I pressed my thumbs and forefingers together to make a closed loop and proved to my own satisfaction that the card wasn't suspended from an invisible thread. Then I stepped back and ran a full spectrum scan, checking for magnetic fields, static electrical charge, anything that could explain what I was seeing. Finally, the card began to tremble, and then it fluttered to the floor, just missing Spot's nose. The dog snorted again.

Sorry, Art transmitted. *I can only manage light weights for short periods but I've never been that interested in levitation. A few of us who have kept at it since we occupied these bodies can move stones around, but in the end, it's not the most useful skill in the world. After all, it takes less energy to just bend over and pick up the stone.*

"So what's the area of magic that's worth all of this effort on your part? Is it the ability to infiltrate computing systems?"

Art waved a hand dismissively. *I can't imagine anything more boring than snooping around in the crude computing infrastructure of less advanced species, and there's nothing we need from them in any case. The highest purpose of magic is to alter the space-time continuum.*

"Like the transfer crystals created by the mages of Eniniac," I guessed.

We know that the mages can create a void in a perfect crystal by singing ancient songs, and that the liquid that seeps out of that void will, when cast in the air, create a net around a similar volume of space that will transfer everything captured in its web back to the hollow crystal, wherever it may be. Mastering a similar magical transport mechanism is our own goal because it would allow for the exploration of distant galaxies and perhaps even other universes.

"The return problem," I acknowledged. "We also have the ability to send ourselves places from which we can't get back due to the amount of infrastructure that would have to be recreated, not to mention the increasing targeting errors that occur at intergalactic distances. Physical exploration is that important to you?"

It helps pass the time, Art replied with a shrug. *Do you have something better?*

"Point taken. But why not just buy anchor crystals from the mages? Sure, they're the most expensive objects in our League and the mages don't make many of them, but compared to the time and money you're investing…"

Time and money are of no importance to entities as old as ourselves. It's the process that matters.

Seventeen

"I don't get why you insisted on moving the meeting out back when we have a perfectly good dining room and bar area," I complained to Sue, as I helped her spread a tablecloth over the row of picnic tables. "Talking is thirsty work."

"eBeth and Peter are underage, or at least, they would be back on Earth, and I don't understand why you invited Pffift to our team meeting."

"I thought you liked Pffift."

"I do, Mark, but as your second-in-command, I have to say that your approach to operational security has become—" she paused for a moment as if searching for the right word—"puzzling."

"That's because everybody on this planet seems to know more about what's going on than we do," I told her. "The Originals aren't only spying on us, they're spying on the humans who are spying on us. It's a breach of ethics."

"Spy ethics?" she asked, at the same time directing Helen to place the tray of fresh-baked cookies in the center of the table. Stacey and Paul followed, carrying between them the wheeled service cart that would have had rough going on the grass, which I now noticed needed cutting. Sometimes I wished I was back on Earth living in a government-subsidized apartment where the upkeep wasn't my responsibility. "Put the lemonade and the iced tea on the

table, and make sure everybody has a plate," Sue instructed the couple.

"Pffift knows more about what's going on with Earth
and Eniniac than we do," I continued, "and I doubt he'd be
taking all the risks he does if he didn't have strong support
at League headquarters."

"At least we have them all beat on Library," Paul said,
producing a bottle of single malt Scotch and placing it on
the table. "That's my seat."

"Are we late?" Kim asked, entering the backyard
through the side gate. Justin trailed behind her like a good
husband, carrying a large bowl of what turned out to be
twelve bean salad. I couldn't have named all of the different beans on a bet. "I looked in the window and the
grandfather clock in the bar is showing five past," she
added.

"Sue set it fifteen minutes fast to encourage our customers to go home early," I told her. "Plus, it brings me a
little extra business in watch repair because everybody
thinks they're running slow."

"All we're missing for the perfect vegetarian picnic is
potato salad, and Peter is bringing that," Sue said, survey-
ing the table with satisfaction.

"Peter cooks?" Stacey asked. "I thought he ate all of his
meals here or at the baker's."

"Potato salad isn't really cooking and eBeth is helping
him. What's that smell?"

"Surprise," Pffift said, coming around the corner of The
Eatery on the other side of the yard. "I brought pizza."

"Where did you get pizza on this planet?" I demanded.

"I stocked up on frozen food while I was on Earth and
brought these down in the gig. The baker next door let me
use his oven in exchange for the recipe. When I translated

197

the ingredients list for him, I left out all of the preservatives and artificial flavorings, so I'm betting whatever he comes up with will be pretty good."

"I'll take those," I said to Pffift, reaching over the fence. "Come in through the house or go around to the other side."

"Wow, this is shaping up to be a real picnic," eBeth enthused, leading Peter into the yard. "I should have invited my students."

"Let's not stand on formalities," Sue said. "Everybody grab a seat and dig in."

"I seem to be getting hungrier every day," Stacey told Kim. "My encounter suit diagnostics don't show any problems, but maybe you could program up an appetite suppressant algorithm before I need diet pills."

"That makes no sense at all," I told her. "You don't digest food, and as long as you rinse out your holding tank, you won't gain any weight."

"She meant it metaphorically," Justin told me. I was trying to figure out how metaphors were relevant to encounter suit mechanics when Pffift reached the table, having entered through the front of The Eatery and emerged from the rear.

"You have a lovely garden, Sue," the Hanker complimented my second-in-command. "Those flowers are gorgeous and they smell almost as good as the pizza. I don't suppose Mark helped."

"I don't think he's even noticed," Sue said, and I caught an overtone of sadness in her voice.

"I'm out here every day," I protested. "This garden cuts down on our grocery bill and the patrons can tell the difference between a tomato picked five minutes ago and one that was delivered first thing in the morning."

"They're talking about the flowers, Mark," eBeth informed me.

"Flowers are critical to attracting insects to carry pollen to the stigma so that the fruits and vegetables can develop. I'm a big fan."

"Over three years in that encounter suit and you still haven't learned how to appreciate the beauty of flowers," Pffift said, helping himself to a large slice of his own pizza. "Oh, that's hot."

"I'll bet I'm more human than you are," I challenged him.

"You're on," the Hanker replied immediately, and the fact that he took another bite of the pizza even though he had just burned the roof of his mouth told me that I was probably in trouble. "What did you score on the test?"

"What test?"

"You didn't take a human test when you put on the encounter suit?"

"I don't even know what a human test is."

"I want to take it," eBeth said. "Is it multiple choice?"

"It is, actually," Pffift replied, shaking a ruggedized tablet out of the crudely-fashioned man-purse he insisted on passing off as a shoulder bag. He looked at his fingers, which were already greasy from the pizza, and pushed the tab in eBeth's direction with his elbow. "You do it. The password is 1679."

"Is everything with you the Arecibo message?" I demanded.

"It's one less thing to remember," Pffift said unapologetically. "Tap the little icon of the maze with the rat and the cheese, eBeth."

"Eat first," Sue urged her.

"I can do both," eBeth said, and taking a slice of pizza in one hand, navigated to the human test icon with the other. "You're the high scorer, Pffift?"

"Ninety," the Hanker boasted. "Of course, I watched a lot of your satellite TV before I ever set foot on Earth."

"Who are all these scores in the twenties?"

"Some of my crew insisted on trying it. How can anybody score under twenty-five when there are only four choices per question? Losers," he concluded. "And don't read any of the questions out loud because I only paid for enough to take the test once."

"Where do you buy such a thing, Pffift?" Kim asked.

"Back on Earth, the dark web. I think somebody ripped it off from a psychology textbook but I wasn't motivated enough to investigate."

I tried not to look nervous as eBeth flew through the test with one finger, alternately scrolling down and clicking multiple choice buttons, but I was already regretting that I never took her advice to read less and watch more TV myself. The potato salad was edible, the twelve bean salad was delicious, and the cookies had raisins, so I avoided them.

"Done," eBeth announced. "Ninety-eight."

"Very impressive," Pffift said, though I thought he sounded a little disappointed at getting beaten so handily. "Pass it to Mark."

"I am human, you know," the girl told him. "If the test was really that accurate, I would have gotten a hundred."

"I want to try," Sue declared, intercepting the tablet as it was passed down the table.

"You're going to kill it," Helen told her. "You're the most human AI that I know. And I got next."

"I'm trusting you all not to feed answers to Mark," Pffift said. "That includes, radio frequency, infrared, quantum—"

"I'm not going to cheat, Pffift," I interrupted him.

"And that's how I already know I'm going to beat you," the Hanker said. "A human would cheat without even thinking about it."

"Done," Sue announced, in half the time eBeth had taken. "Ooh, I got a hundred!"

eBeth high-fived my second-in-command, and the tablet passed to Helen, who barely seemed to look at the questions before answering. My nerves were starting to go and I nodded at Paul to pour me a stiff drink from his bottle of Scotch.

"Pressure," Pffift sang under his breath. I was really beginning to hate the Hanker.

"What did you guys bet?" Peter asked.

"If I win, he has to let us use the portal for Earth tourism," Pffift answered without hesitation.

"We didn't agree on anything, and the whole team has to vote on that," I told him.

"I'm good with it," Stacey said, followed by a chorus of me-too's that covered everybody present. Spot even joined in with a friendly bark.

"Then free dinner whenever I'm here," Pffift offered.

"You just said the bet was for portal usage," I objected.

"And you said it wasn't."

"Ninety-seven," Helen announced her results. "If those questions about pets had been about baking, I would have aced it. I've never had a pet."

"Let me see it," I said, unable to keep the note of doom from my voice as I accepted the tablet.

"Don't think, just go with your first instinct," eBeth advised me.

I braced myself and tapped on the maze, getting a flash screen showing the high scorers before the questions began.

"You're moving your lips while you read," Pffift observed. "Maybe you're going to do better at this than I thought."

"Don't distract him," Sue defended me. "Try the lemonade. I just came from Earth and the lieutenant let me raid the storeroom for sugar."

"I've never been through an observer team portal," the Hanker said. "Do they have the same filter limits on manufactured goods?"

"You can always use Rynxian cloaking technology if you've got a lot of stuff," Paul told him. "It's not the full filter set that you get on the regular network portals."

"What do you want to bring to Earth?" eBeth asked the Hanker. "I mean, the hand-crafted goods here are nice and everything, but it's not that different from back home. People there only buy the factory-made stuff because it's cheaper."

"I want to bring some cloth samples that I picked up on the way here from Eniniac," Pffift explained. "We did a business assessment of Earth while we were there and concluded that there's money to be made in the garment industry."

"You want to sell clothes made of alien materials to people?"

Pffift spit a spray of lemonade out of his mouth as he failed to suppress his body's natural reaction, and I accidentally clicked the wrong multiple-choice button as I attempted to wipe the screen clear.

"You have it backwards," the Hanker told the girl when he regained his composure. "One thing Earth has in common with the rest of the galaxy is that the garment industry is always seeking lower production costs. I'm talking about the low-end, here. Your planet doesn't have the machines in place to work with any of the technologically advanced fabrics, but most species prefer natural fibers in their sensitive areas, and I'm betting we can turn Earth into the underwear capital of the galaxy within a century."

"Won't that be bad for Earth's economy?" Peter asked. "I heard that all of those overseas factories barely pay their workers, and the buildings are fire traps."

"Don't worry about that. Any factory that exports to League worlds has to follow League standards, which includes not chaining the doors of fire exits. What passes as cheap labor rates on the galactic scale will seem like riches to anybody who's currently working in one of those sweatshops."

"But if everybody quits working at making human clothes for better paying jobs making alien underwear, what will people wear?" Peter followed up.

"Intelligent question," Pffift said, and eBeth beamed at her boyfriend. "My theory is that rising prices are what lift an economy. When people in your country are willing to pay, say, a hundred dollars for a pair of jeans, you'll find no shortage of locals willing to open businesses making jeans and paying their employees good wages. But if everybody on the planet would rather earn money making alien lingerie, you can always import high-tech alternatives or just go naked. It's a pretty warm planet most of the time."

"What high-tech alternatives?" eBeth asked.

"Lots of species use spray-on clothing. You just make your color choice and hit the button before getting out of the shower in the morning. Of course, it works better for bodies without hair," he added thoughtfully.

"Okay," I said. "I'm finished, but you cost me at least one answer by spitting lemonade on the screen and the conversation was distracting. Everybody looked at me expectantly and I hit the 'Score me' button. "Eighty-four."

Pffift pumped his fist in the air, and Paul reached across the table with the bottle and poured me another drink.

"A middle-B is nothing to be ashamed of, Mark," Sue consoled me. "Just imagine if you had taken the test a year ago."

"I don't get it," I grumbled. "I thought that everybody liked me."

"They do," Pffift said. "How many humans do you know who don't have any enemies? You're too nice." He got up and came over to where I sat, and for a moment I thought he was patting me on the shoulder, but then I realized he was just wiping the pizza grease off his fingers before taking back the tab. "Let's see, just as I expected. You blew all five questions related to selflessness. If you'd ever been in a human war, you would have gotten killed in the first battle."

"I think his willingness to sacrifice himself for others is sweet," Sue said.

"But it puts him at the end of the bell curve," Pffift explained. "Passing as human isn't about being better than the average man on the street. Too good isn't good at this game."

"I've got flaws," I argued. "Just before you came, Sue was pointing out that I've been ignoring operational security protocols and putting personal relationships before the mission."

"That's why you scored as well as you did despite being such a choirboy. Listen, take me to Earth and I'll buy a new set of questions. Six points isn't that big of a deal on a standardized test. We'll treat today as a practice run."

"He can have my place," eBeth volunteered. "I'm not in any hurry to go back and I don't want to lose a day of teaching."

"I don't think Justin or I need anything," Kim said. "Maybe a couple of magazines if you happen to be near a newsstand. I'm considering submitting a journal article about Earth's pharmaceutical advertisements but I haven't been keeping up lately."

"You may as well go before Pffift's ship returns with official representatives from the reservation worlds," Sue suggested. "Helen and I can take care of The Eatery while you're gone."

"Bring back some games," Helen said. "I'm going to hack that 'My Life' editing station to project streaming video."

"What if the villagers don't want to watch you, eBeth, and Peter slaying monsters?" I asked.

"We'll play at night," eBeth said. "Art is the only one who hangs out in the Ferrymen Temple after dark, and he's cool."

I shook my head, wondering if the locals would one day remember me as the devil who introduced snakes to the Garden of Eden.

"You know," Pffift said, looking up from the tab he was still studying, "you got the last six questions in a row wrong."

"Where they changed from showing the answers below the question to above?" I asked. "I thought about checking the code, but the programming is so crude I was worried I'd see the answers by mistake."

"It's not programming, it's scripting," the Hanker said. "Oops, I thought I fixed that. After a few tests, the buffer tends to overflow because I don't reset any of the variables when the script launches."

"Where did you learn how to write script?" eBeth asked him in disgust. "Even I know better than that."

"Hey, I never even had one of these things in my hands before landing on Earth. I'm still having trouble figuring out the difference between the operating system and the advertisements."

"That's on purpose," I told him. "Humans are tricky that way."

"Well, you were choosing from the wrong row of buttons for your last six answers, though that's reason enough to fail you right there," Pffift said. "If you had put the answers in the right places, you would have scored —damn it."

"Ninety?" Sue asked, and the Hanker nodded in confirmation. "You see, Mark. You're just as human as Pffift."

"He's still not alive," the disappointed alien mumbled.

"What do you mean?" eBeth demanded. "Mark's as alive as you or me."

"I don't have a biological cell in my body, other than what I eat or inhale," I told her. "Pffift is just being a sore tie-er. It doesn't bother me. Artificial intelligence doesn't judge its worth by biological standards."

"But you said that the Originals are AI, and they're biological."

"The Originals are something I've never encountered before," I admitted. "Art told me they took on biological forms specifically to practice magic, though they're also on vacation."

"Do you think they'd be interested in some learning materials?" Pffift asked.

"I thought you told me that the Regent of Eniniac suggested you stock up and you didn't fall for it."

"I didn't fall for it, but I bought a few things," the Hanker said. "Do you really think I'm going to defy the wife of the Archmage over a potential inventory problem? I took a couple crates of nursery-school-for-mages kits, though they're still on my ship since I didn't think there was going to be a market for them here. I planned to unload it on the humans when I stopped at Earth to pick up the next shipment of tennis balls."

"You think that humans can learn magic?" I asked him.

"No. What does that have to do with anything?"

I have to admit, sales was never my strong suit.

Eighteen

"I'm sure Mark told us that the portal filters prevent the system from being used to move trade goods in order to protect the galactic shipping industry," Saul cautioned the Hanker. "It's going to be a tight squeeze as it is."

"There's an exception for commercial samples carried by salesmen," Pffift replied. "And it's a portal, not a closet. Did you think we were all going to cram in there like college kids in a phone booth?"

"What's a phone booth?" eBeth asked.

"Before your time," I told her. "Pffift must have seen one in a movie."

"What are we waiting for?" the Hanker demanded. "This pack is heavier than it looks and the belt is cutting off circulation to my lower brain."

"Sue decided to come with us and she'll be here momentarily. She spent the whole night baking for the children who used to be in her daycare."

"Here she is now," eBeth said, as my second-in-command started up the stairs. "I've got to get to school, but you guys have a good time, stay out of trouble, and don't forget what I told you about looking both ways before crossing the street. Spot, that applies to you too."

The dog gave a tail thump, his standard answer to instructions addressed in his direction that didn't involve coming and eating. My artificial salivary glands began working overtime as Sue topped the stairs with a giant picnic basket full of fresh-baked cakes and cookies, and I couldn't help thinking about Pavlov's dog. Something was definitely wrong with my encounter suit, and I made another mental note to get it checked out on Library. My stack of mental notes was threatening to overflow.

"Stop procrastinating and open the portal already," Pffift said. "Some of us have important business on Earth."

"I was just working out the intra-dimensional math," I lied, pulling open the closet door and issuing the command code. "Before we—" Spot brushed by my legs and jumped through, followed by the Hanker, whose giant backpack cleared a nice path for Sue to follow with her basket. Saul and Joshua looked at me expectantly.

"Go ahead," I told them, feeling more like the doorman than a mission commander. "I'll bring up the rear."

The headmaster paused in the closet and asked, "Why does Earth look like a small office that hasn't been dusted in years?"

"The other end is in the basement of my old restaurant and the foundation needs repointing," I told him. "Go."

Joshua stepped through the portal, followed closely by Saul. I grabbed Pffift's second pack of fabric samples by the straps, and pulling the closet door closed behind me, joined them in my old office. Pffift had already started for the stairs, and Spot was likely ahead of him.

Saul's first words to me after stepping through an intra-dimensional portal to the homeworld of his ancestors were, "I know some good bricklayers if you want this fixed."

"The foundation has lasted over a hundred years and gravity is working in our favor," I told him. "Could you grab my phone for me?"

"Your what?"

"The little shiny thing lying on the desk with the black cord running to the—never mind, I'll get it," I said. "Sue, can you show these two upstairs and I'll be with you in a minute?"

I unplugged the charger, swiped through the lockscreen, and groaned. Two-hundred and fourteen messages! I could see from a glance that they were all from old customers of my computer repair business who must have heard a rumor that I was back from Australia. I slung Pffift's extra pack over one shoulder, closed the portal, locked the office door, and hurried to catch up with the others.

"And this is a television," I heard the lieutenant explaining slowly in an unnaturally loud voice. "Tel-e-vis-ion."

"Like a 'My Life' editing station," the headmaster said. "Did you get everything, Saul?"

"This translation device is amazing," the safety inspector marveled. "I can even understand what the little people trapped in the box are saying."

"What's he speaking?" the lieutenant asked. "It sounds a little like the weird language those brothers with the food truck are always yelling at each other. Good falafel, though."

"Joshua speaks some English but I brought you a translator so you can understand Saul," I told him, putting my phone on the bar and pulling out another ear-cuff translator. "I just programmed it this morning so you're the guinea pig."

The lieutenant accepted the device I handed him and placed it over his ear. "Somebody say something in alien," he demanded.

"It's not alien. It's a mishmash of Aramaic and ancient Mediterranean languages, just like your English grew out of German with major borrowings from Romance languages," I informed him.

"I hate to tell you, but you've got that wrong, Mark," the lieutenant said. "Everybody knows that English is from the Latin. It's even an expression."

"Very pleased to meet you," Saul interrupted in his native tongue. Obviously, he knew the start of a pointless argument when he heard one and had decided to head it off at the pass. "May I ask the time of day?"

"It's ten o'clock in the morning and we won't be opening for lunch for another hour so you showed up at a good time," the lieutenant replied, again speaking loudly and over-enunciating his words. "Are you hungry?" He pantomimed spooning invisible food into his mouth and making exaggerated eating sounds.

"They're aliens, Bob, or technically speaking, foreigners," I told the lieutenant. "They're not hard of hearing."

"But this is how they trained us to speak to aliens at the special seminar the state made everybody attend after the big incident a couple months back."

"What incident?"

"With the alien tourists. Man, were they angry," he recalled with a chuckle.

"I appreciate the effort," Saul said diplomatically. "I don't mean to rush anybody, but I'm anxious to see the world outside and I understand that you're starting a travel business. Do you have an itinerary for us?"

"I thought we'd wing it the first time and just go wherever you want," the lieutenant replied. "I'll be guiding you myself and then you can return the favor back on Reservation."

"Excuse me?" I cut in. "You were planning on going back with us?"

"My clients are in a hurry so we can talk about it later. You'll be here to open the portal next Tuesday at ten?"

"I'll make sure he doesn't forget," Sue said, which, given how many balls I had in the air, was both wise and generous of her. "And I'll see you back home, Mark. I don't want to miss snack time at Lilly's daycare."

My second-in-command gave me a quick peck on the cheek and followed the lieutenant and our two beta-tourists out of the restaurant. Pffift winked, slipped behind the bar, and helped himself to a shot on his new business partner's tab.

"Looks like it's just me and you," he said happily. "I'm not in any particular hurry to head to the train station."

"You're taking a train somewhere?"

"To the closest major train station with a portal," he replied. "Then it's off to the waystation, and then back to Earth again in the Far East. I'm planning on visiting factories in China, Bangladesh, Indonesia, India and Vietnam."

"You're planning on racking up hundreds of light years running back and forth through portals to travel a few thousand miles on Earth?"

"I told you that flying on this world is miserable, unless you go first class, and I'm not paying five times as much to arrive a fraction of a second before a couple hundred people sitting a few rows behind me. Your engineers made the smart call putting the portals in train stations because they go everywhere I need to visit in the countries with the sewing machines."

"How convenient for you," I muttered. "Are you planning on dragging both packs?"

"I'm going to leave one here and come back for it when I start running out of samples," Pffift told me. "Unless you want to tag along, that is."

"Maybe next trip. I want to return to Reservation and spend more time with Art before the negotiating teams from the other two reservation worlds arrive. I have the feeling that I'm missing something in all of this."

"Do you have time to drive me to the spaceport? The lieutenant always uses the Jeep that young Peter left behind so we can take the company car."

"The closest spaceport to here is more than a thousand miles away and it takes them years to schedule a launch," I said. "What would you do at a spaceport anyway?"

"I want to check on my spaceport, at the old mall. You really are having trouble with your memory, aren't you?"

"Just because you brought down a lander a few times doesn't make it a spaceport," I argued. "You need a lot of infrastructure, not to mention government permission at more levels than you can imagine."

"Guess again," Pffift said, adjusting the position of his pack and pulling a keychain from a peg beside the cash register. Apparently he really had spent a good chunk of his time on Earth hanging out with the lieutenant and hatching plans. "The railroad spur to my spaceport should be finished by now. The federal government granted us extraterritorial status and a few other perks in exchange for returning everybody's gold. I went with all prefab construction for the buildings."

"You returned all the Swiss gold and invested your own money to improve the property? That doesn't sound like you."

"The tennis ball contract pays big bucks and I needed somewhere to store them," Pffift explained. "Governments around here don't work that badly as long as you promise to create a lot of jobs. I even got a fifty-year remission on property taxes."

"You just said the spaceport was granted extraterritorial status!"

"All the more reason not to get in trouble with the locals," the Hanker remarked as he followed me out the door. "You better drive. I never got the hang of dodging all of the idiots on the road."

"That's the company car?" I asked, staring at my old van, which still had 'www.ifitbreaks.com' on the side. "All you did was cut the top line off of my magnetic sign. Why did you keep my website address?"

"You let the domain name expire so I picked it up cheap. We're using it for the tourism business."

"You couldn't have come up with something that had 'travel' in the name?"

"All of the good ones were taken."

Spot ran past us towards the van, and knowing that he would claim the passenger seat, I maliciously beeped the cargo door open. The dog hopped in and I climbed into the driver's seat while Pffift struggled out of his pack and set it in the back. The Hanker came around to the passenger door, opened it, and smiled at the dog.

"You know," he said conversationally. "Humans call where you're sitting the death seat."

Spot yawned, settled into a curled up position, and pretended to fall asleep.

"Just get in the back," I told Pffift. "It's not a long ride."

"You mean, in the back with all the food?" the Hanker asked with exaggerated innocence. "The lieutenant keeps telling those kids that the van isn't a storeroom, but it looks like somebody never brought in—"

Spot was through the space between the seats and into the back before Pffift could finish his sentence. A few seconds later I heard him tearing into a package.

"If those are pretzels, go easy," I called over my shoulder. "You know too much salt isn't good for you."

"That sounded more like potato chips," Pffift said, as he climbed into the passenger seat. "I couldn't believe how many bags a day this place goes through."

I'd long since learned that Spot could eat anything without getting sick, and I figured that cleaning up after the dog would teach the current employees a lesson about leaving food in the van overnight. Checking the mirrors, I backed out of the spot next to the dumpster and headed for the old mall.

Pffift chatted about his plans for the world's garment industry as I drove, and I have to admit that he had done his homework. Given the piece rates he planned on paying, which were more than double the current standard for illegal compensation schemes, I wondered that the Hankers hadn't tried setting up a Ferrymen-style operation themselves.

"It's no good without the portals," he told me, as if speaking to a child.

"What does instantaneous travel have to do with anything?" I asked. "It's a decidedly low-tech industry, and you can't bring commercial quantities through the portals."

"Have you ever heard of fast fashion?" Pffift asked in return, casting a sidelong glance in my direction.

Rather than admitting my ignorance, I looked it up on Wikipedia. "You're setting up a copycat operation? You told everybody you were going to become the underwear king!"

"You want me to pay well, don't you? Copycat fashions pay much better than the commodity stuff, even in the underwear business, but every day counts. The secret is getting the new designs to the factory within twenty-four hours of a show. The rest is about moving the product to market before it's saturated."

"Why did I think you actually had something honest in mind?"

"It's a grey area," Pffift said. "It's not like we're stealing the actual designs, it's more like our own interpretation. They wouldn't think twice about it on Reservation."

"And what about League copyright law?"

"I leave that to our legal team. My plan is to ignore the home markets and go after the periphery, which is under-served by the fashion industry. It's almost like we're doing a public service."

"Did you have a particular species in mind?"

"We'll just rotate through everybody according to the fashion calendar," Pffift said. "With any luck, they won't even notice—look at that!" he interrupted himself, pointing at the graceful tower rising off to the side of the state highway that marked the beginning of the mall property. "When I told my grandson I wanted a statement building along the lines of the Eiffel Tower, I didn't expect him to take me literally."

"Looks like you aren't the only copycat in the family," I said with a grin. "You really left your grandson behind? I thought he was just a kid."

"That was hundreds of years ago, Mark. Your sense of time is pretty bad for a clockmaker."

"Is that a hangar?" I asked, indicating an enormous building that looked like a Quonset hut on steroids. "Are you planning on doing ground maintenance?"

216

"It's a warehouse, cheapest design I could find that wouldn't collapse under a snow load," Pffift said. "They really should do something about controlling the weather on this planet."

"It doesn't look very inviting," I remarked as we took the old mall exit and were forced to stop by a high gate. "The chain-link fence goes all the way around?"

"The government insisted," the Hanker said, rolling down the window and waving at the armed guard who was approaching the van. "Personally, I think some congressman's brother-in-law owns a fence factory, but they kept making noise about invasive species and this was the compromise."

"Didn't you explain that your ships are equipped with systems that prevent invasive species from stowing away in the cargo?" I asked as the gate began rolling open.

"I even loaned them a detection unit for testing and never heard back," Pffift said. "My guess is that they tried to take it apart and they're too embarrassed to ask for another one after it self-destructed."

"That sounds like the way the government works, except for the embarrassed part."

"Except I warned them like a hundred times that it's a sealed unit with no user-serviceable parts and that it would melt into slag if they tried removing the cover. It will take humans a while to figure out that the rest of the galaxy protects its technology with self-destruct mechanisms."

"Still, it's a chain-link fence," I said as I drove through the gate. "Maybe it would stop invasive cattle, but I'm not betting on it."

"Head over to the warehouse. I want to see how the inventory is coming along."

Pffift scowled as we pulled in next to a Lamborghini, the roof of which didn't come up to the door handles of my old van.

"Are you sure you returned all the gold?" I asked.

"All the gold that we didn't burn running billionaires back and forth to Mars," the Hanker told me with a sly grin. "At least, that's how my accountant made the math work out."

"So you never actually used the faster-than-light drive you sold the humans?"

"Don't look at me like that. We delivered a faster-than-light drive that runs on gold to the humans and we took them on a few jaunts around the solar system. I never specifically said that the drive was active for those trips, only that it was operational. There's a difference you know. Look the words up if you don't believe me."

A handsome young man hurried up to greet us as we climbed out of the van. "Hey, Gramps," he addressed Pffift. "Long time no see. Who's the new chauffeur?"

"This is Mark, from Library," the Hanker said. "He's playing an important role in getting our new business off the ground."

"Artificial intelligence. Cool."

"He's as human as I am," Pffift told his grandson. "We scored the same on the test."

"You mean five points below me?" the kid said. He whipped out a smartphone and brought up his own version of the human test to show off his score. "And I didn't even study."

"Nice tower," I interjected to change the subject before my friend lost his patience. "I hear you've been putting in a railroad spur as well."

"It's all finished, on time and under budget," the young Hanker boasted. "Speaking of which, I gave myself a bonus."

"How much?" Pffift demanded, glancing at the Lamborghini.

"Half of the money I saved. You have to admit that's fair. Come on, I'll show you everything I've done."

"Don't ever have grandchildren," Pffift muttered out of the side of his mouth as the kid led us into the warehouse.

"I'd have to have children first," I reminded him.

"And you're waiting for marriage?"

"It's just an encounter suit, Pffift. I can't use it to father offspring with Sue."

"But you want to," the Hanker said, making it a statement rather than a question.

"Fork a process," his grandson contributed over his shoulder, as if AI reproduction was the easiest thing in the world. "How tough can it be?"

"I've never actually done it before so I couldn't tell you," I admitted. "I better get back to the portal, Pffift. I'm starting to feel weird."

"Fast respiration, sweaty palms, the haunted look in your eyes. You're having a panic attack," he informed me. "Haven't you and Sue ever discussed this before?"

"Not in so many words," I said. "Give me a second to run a self-diagnostic."

"Well?" Pffift demanded a second later.

"There's nothing wrong with the suit," I reported, even though my knees felt weak.

"If talking about having kids freaks you out, you should have scored better on the human test," the grandson observed. "I'll get you a glass of water."

"Thanks," I said, activating Kim's inebriation algorithm and examining the underlying code. By the time the kid returned, I had determined that the easiest work-around was to simply knock two carbons and four hydrogens off the algorithm's match for an ethyl alcohol molecule. Man, that water hit the spot.

Nineteen

"Are you sure you don't want to come out here and join the rest of us?" I addressed my words to the dense foliage at the back of the Ferrymen Temple. "It's not like everybody doesn't know you're in there."

"Double negative," eBeth hissed at me, and then tried her own hand at coaxing the Original out of hiding. "Come on, Art. Don't you want a voice in the negotiations?"

Mark can speak for us, Art transmitted.

"He says I can speak for them," I told eBeth.

"Shake a bush if you really told him that," she said.

"You don't trust me?" I asked as a plant resembling a giant fern rustled energetically.

"I'm just trying to engage him," eBeth whispered. "Psychology 101."

"Saul is here," I tried, hoping this would tempt him out. "You know, the safety officer who protects the privacy of the Originals in the county?"

Saul is the president of the Council of Spaceports, Art shot back. *Playing a safety officer was just his cover story to come and keep an eye on you. He grew up locally and has a vacation cottage at the lake.*

"If you two are done talking with the shrubbery I'd like to get this meeting under way," Pffift called loudly from the front of the hall. "If Art wants to come out, he knows we won't eat him."

"A member of this planet's indigenous species?" the head representative from the closer of the two other reservation worlds asked Saul.

"Yes and no," Saul replied. "I'll fill you in later, it gets confusing."

"So let's just jump right in and get started," the Hanker declared, climbing up on the stage next to the 'My Life' editing station. "I'm Pffift, and those of you who just arrived from the other reservation worlds have already enjoyed the hospitality of my ship and crew. May I assume that you enjoyed your trip?"

"Abiferry," a tall, square-jawed woman introduced herself. "Your crew cheats at cards and they don't pay up when they lose."

"But the food was excellent," the bearded man accompanying her added. "And it was fascinating to watch your medical technicians grow new human body parts in your vats."

"If you really want to see something, you'll have to stay around to watch them put a whole person together," Pffift said, choosing to ignore the gambling complaints. "And the gentleman in the silk pajamas?"

"Zhang," the leader of the other delegation identified himself. "Our accommodations were adequate and we arrived on time."

"Excellent. Now how many cargo loads of merchandise a year do each of you plan to ship?"

"Aren't we going a bit fast, Pffift?" I interrupted. "The off-world delegates just arrived, and they can only be aware of the broad contours of the deal we've hashed out for their approval."

"I took the liberty of having my executive officer brief them as soon as the ship came within communications range," the Hanker brushed aside my complaint.

"I've had a chance to speak with my colleagues before the meeting and we're all in agreement," Saul added. "Branching out into new markets under our own branding is something we've been discussing for decades."

"Is that so?" demanded a screechy voice from the rear of the Ferrymen Temple.

Everybody spun around to stare at the tall lizard-creature who stalked forward on his hind legs, a long tail held high behind him to keep everything in balance. The Ferryman wore a virtual reality visor of the multi-purpose type affected by their senior officers, which means it wasn't limited to viewing entertainment content and playing games. He was accompanied by four lower-caste Ferry-men, all of whom wore less expensive versions of the same visor. One of the lizards carried a metal box with him, and if I'm any judge of reptilian lower-facial expressions, they all looked angry.

Paul, I've got Ferrymen here! I transmitted to my technical specialist.

Sorry about that. I took the grid offline a few hours ago to redistribute the detectors farther from the base station to improve the accuracy. I hired Pffift's crew to deliver the units after they dropped off the delegates this morning.

"We are honored by your presence, O Sky Gods," Saul greeted the newcomers with a polite bow. "We were just discussing the possibility of bringing you—"

"Spare me your stories," the Ferryman chief interrupted him. "There's a cloaked Hanker exploration and exploitation vessel in orbit that we almost ran into when exiting hyperspace, and that fellow," he paused to point at yours truly, "is clearly an AI wearing a human encounter suit. Observer team?" he guessed.

"On special assignment," I admitted.

"We're in for fifteen percent on the new venture?" the lizard-man continued, spinning back to Saul.

"Actually, we thought that for business we developed independently, you might waive—"

"Fifteen percent," the Ferryman repeated, nodding in agreement with himself. "But we aren't here about your backdoor deals. Do any of you remember the one special favor we asked?"

"You were looking for an old holographic drama titled 'Kingdom of the Desert,'" Abiferry replied immediately. "One of our ships, I mean, one of your ships crewed by our people, was approached by a seller while stopping at a Bintrid orbital facility for scheduled maintenance. In accordance with your requisition, they were able to obtain the complete archive."

"Paying with our credit," the Ferryman hissed. "Fifteen million gal-creds, not counting shipping and handling to our location at the time. Does that ring a bell?"

"The sum was within the budget you had authorized," the tall woman replied strongly. "The captain handled the transaction himself, and the presence of every episode of the drama was verified by a bonded entertainment agent. If there's any problem—"

"Just a little matter of encryption preventing us from opening any episodes beyond the first season. The series is all there, yes, but we can't watch 99.99% of it!"

I saw my chance to conciliate the angry aliens and jumped in. "It's not really our thing to interfere with legal content protection schemes, but maybe I can make an exception." If the Ferrymen were going to step on the new deal for fifteen percent, the whole thing might fall apart, including our tourism-to-Earth startup.

The chief gestured at his subordinate who was carrying the metal box. It was a Bintrid high-capacity storage unit with entertainment-level encryption, but cracking codes was an old hobby of mine, and I activated the holographic interface. A moment later I was lost in a maze of fractal-like patterns that seemed to stretch towards eternity. I'm not sure how long I spent fumbling for the end of a thread before a three-fingered hand gripped my shoulder.

It's trickier than it looks, Art informed me. *Let's bring it outside where all of my clones can see the patterns. If my mind wasn't so piecemeal I could crack the code almost instantly, but these latency issues are a nightmare.*

"Our friend wants the storage unit brought outside where his clones can see the hologram," I informed the Ferrymen. "The Originals on this world are actually a limited number of artificial intelligence entities who have spread their minds over large numbers of biological hosts for the sake of the experience."

"Yes, they're here on vacation," the Ferryman chief said impatiently, signaling his subordinate to carry the metal cube outside. "We never would have created a reservation on the planet if they had been natives. Their mega-art is remarkable."

"What does he mean by that?" I asked Art as we followed the storage unit back down the aisle.

Haven't you ever seen this world from space? the Original countered my question.

"No. It's all been portals with me." When we stepped outside, there were hundreds of hairy knuckle-draggers milling around on the village common. I noticed a few with different physical characteristics mixed in, and Art confirmed my conjecture.

A few of my compatriots wished to monitor the conference, he replied. *But first things first.*

Every shaggy head swiveled to stare at the swirling holographic lock on the storage unit and a swell of organically produced radio frequency chatter went up that was almost disruptive to my own processing. Then the lock abruptly shattered, and the only thing left was a half-translucent silvery cord tied around the cube like a gift bow.

You see? Art demanded. *This is exactly what I was talking about.*

"Did something go wrong?" I asked. "I thought you broke the encryption cleanly."

We did. The piece that remains is magical protection. It's well beyond my meager skills.

"Not getting anything here," the Ferryman chief said ominously, tapping his visor. "Maybe a twenty-five percent share in the new business would motivate you to be more careful about spending our money in the future."

"It turns out there's also magical protection and it's apparently a powerful enchantment," I explained. "I'm afraid there's nothing further we can do."

The Ferrymen all went rigid, and for a moment I thought they were just drama-withdrawal crazed enough to try something untoward. Then I reached out to sample their feed and discovered that they were all immersed in the first episode of the second season. I looked back to the storage unit and saw the dog greedily licking the surface from which the magical protection had vanished.

"Stop it, Spot," eBeth commanded. "You don't know where that's been."

"It's never prevented him from licking anything before," I told her. "I think we just lucked out."

"What are they all doing?" she asked.

"Drama trance," Abiferry told us, coming up and poking the Ferrymen's leader, who remained unresponsive. "Every episode starts with a recap of the previous broadcast and I guess the first installment of a new season is pretty intense."

"Was he exaggerating about the 99.99%? How many episodes could there possibly be?"

"A thousand seasons is a typical run for epic dramas," I told the girl. "The producers need to recover the cost of converting a planet into a virtual holographic studio and bringing in millions of background actors to live there, sometimes for generations, depending on their lifespans. It's the galaxy's largest industry after tourism, which is why the studios go to such lengths to prevent piracy, even on ancient dramas like this."

"Will you get in trouble with Library for breaking the protection?"

"I don't think I did, and it might be out of copyright by now in any case, but the law keeps changing so it's hard to keep track. The last season of 'Kingdom of the Desert' was shot before the Ferrymen started bringing humans to this world."

"This is the first time in my life they've brought one of the ark transports to the surface," Saul said, pointing towards the wooded area outside the village where an enormous silver ship was floating motionless above the tree line. "Terrible timing, though. Our plan was to use that fifteen percent to build a sovereign wealth fund to protect us in the future. If our Sky Gods insist on their regular cut, there's not much point in continuing with the expansion."

The five Ferrymen slumped a little as if somebody had cut their puppet cords, and to my surprise, the chief actually removed his virtual reality visor. He blinked a few times to let his eyes adjust, and sampled the air with his forked tongue before speaking.

"I was sent here as a punishment for authorizing the original purchase of the series without personally confirming the content, but now I will return to our fleet as a hero. Explain your scheme, but be brief. I have important, uh, things awaiting my attention."

"The excess production of our three worlds has exceeded the capacity of your existing distribution networks, O Sky God," Zhang told him. "Pushing more product into the same markets will result in margin deterioration and the commoditization of our luxury exports. If you could negotiate with some of the newer League members—"

"No, no. That's too much bother," the Ferryman interrupted. "Our distribution network and trade treaties were good enough for my ancestors and they're good enough for me. If you want to gamble on chasing new markets, do it on your own time with your own money."

"But if you insist on taking the same cut of our new business…" Saul left the sentence hanging.

"Did I say fifteen percent? I meant ten percent," the Ferryman told him with a dismissive wave. "Now I need to return to the fleet with this storage unit before our people find something else to watch."

"Not having a fleet of our own, we're forced to seek partnerships to expand our business," Saul continued as if his Sky God hadn't spoken. "Of course, if you could provide us with more ships…"

"Five percent," the Ferrymen offered, and I thought he sounded a bit nervous. "We don't find it convenient to make any changes in the ship-leasing arrangement, and we are a bit overcommitted at the present time with bringing along a new species."

"If you could defer compensation until such a time as our new distribution network is established…"

"Two percent, and that's final," the Ferryman said, and I was surprised to see that he was glaring at Art. "Satisfied?"

The Original spread his arms wide, either to indicate that he conceded the point or offering to give the Ferrymen a consolation hug. The five lizard-men did an abrupt about-face and marched off towards their ark, ignoring the crowd of clones mixed in with villagers, most of whom were holding 'My Life' cubes above their heads to capture the action.

"What was that all about?" I asked Art.

Planet rental, he replied. *We were here first, after all.*

And you're just getting around to collecting the rent now?

I changed the deal going forward. We have a couple thousand years of the local coinage saved up that we never spend on anything, and the truth is, we would have paid them for bringing us humans to watch if they had been smart enough to ask. The Ferrymen are too lazy to negotiate properly.

"How did you communicate all that to him?"

"I added the offer to the new season lead-in when the magical lock dissolved. You didn't notice?"

"I'm drawing a blank," I said, trying to remember exactly what had happened. A vague intuition led me to check my sequential memory stream against my internal timer and I realized that almost a full minute was missing. Had I started napping at random times even while standing?

"Perhaps we should head back inside and wrap this up," Saul suggested, apparently unruffled by the sudden arrival and departure of his Sky Gods. "Shall I assume that we owe favors all around for bringing the Ferrymen down to two percent?"

"That was Art's doing," I told him as we headed back into the temple. "Apparently the Ferrymen have been paying the Originals rent for the planet the last couple thousand years, and Art has agreed to waive it going forward."

"Given that we were the ones who actually paid the rent, stopping it will cancel out the two percent of the new business that we'll be setting aside for the Ferrymen," Saul said. "I don't know how to thank you, Art."

Tell him about the magic supplies, the Original prompted me. *We can pay.*

"Art requests that Pffift include magic education materials in a triangle trade route encompassing the reservation worlds, Earth, and Eniniac," I informed Saul and the other representatives. "The Hanker is already committed to travel to the mage's world twice a year, and the Originals can pay for their purchases."

I have a list here, Art added, producing a paper scroll that must have been hidden in his shaggy coat.

"He has a list," I echoed in verbal speech.

"Let me see," Pffift said, taking the scroll and running his finger down the items, all printed in the same neat English that Art had originally used to communicate with me on bar slates. "I have a few of these onboard my ship. If I had followed the Regent of Eniniac's advice on stocking up, I would have had everything, but you know how pushy mages are."

I found myself yet again looking at Spot, who seemed to be nodding in agreement with something, but the last thing I remembered was telling Pffift that Art had a list. If my memory kept glitching like this, I really was going to have to return to Library for a checkup. A quick scan of my to-do list showed that I'd come to this decision over twenty times in the last week. Maybe I'd hold out for fifty.

"We'd like to begin by setting up a distribution network for the species which the Ferrymen have been ignoring," Zhang was telling the Hanker. "Is your ship available for an extended tour?"

"As long as you don't object to a few stops at fabric wholesalers along the way," Pffift replied. "I have a number of factories on Earth under contract to start sewing for me three months from now. Then I load up on tennis balls for Eniniac, and back here again with magical learning materials for our hairy AI friends."

"Can we get a discount off of your standard shipping rates when our objectives coincide in the future?"

"You mean, if I'm going somewhere to pick up a load of fabric or to drop off finished clothes, you want me to give you a break on shipping your handmade luxury goods?" Pffift frowned. "It sounds complicated to me and my cargo would have priority, but if you're that motivated to save a little money, I suppose we can work something out."

"We plan to start slowly," Abiferry told him. "Our people don't work on spec because there's so much labor involved. We'll have plenty of lead time to arrange shipping schedules as orders come in."

Somebody tugged on my sleeve, and seeing that it was eBeth, I let her lead me back to the indoor garden.

"I don't get it," she said quietly. "I remember people back on Earth arguing over the prices of things that were plainly marked, but these guys are making deals that affect whole planets and there's not even a lawyer in the room."

"Pffift is a lawyer," I told her. "All Hanker ship captains have extensive legal training. Zhang, Abiferry and Saul have their staffers here to go over the fine details, but when there's good will on all sides, things can move pretty quickly."

232

"How about Art?" she asked, nodding at the Original who had sat down in one of the pews where he was obviously following the discussion with interest.

"I don't say this often, eBeth, but he may be the smartest sentient I've ever encountered. It's just a feeling, you understand, plus seeing the hundreds of bodies it took to house whatever part of his mind he brought with him on vacation. I don't know how much of this deal is due to his behind-the-scenes manipulations, but I suspect that a higher power is at work here, and it's not any Sky Gods.

Twenty

"The last lesson for this evening is how to order a hamburger," I told my class. "It's a little late to actually eat hamburgers, but my wife has deep-fried the traditional side dish for you to sample, including ketchup imported directly from Earth. Sue?"

My second-in-command passed out paper bowls full of French fries, which had cooled to just about the right temperature on her walk from The Eatery to the village school, where we were all helping teach night courses in Earth tourism. eBeth was handling English, of course, Paul was instructing our potential tourists in street safety with the help of some horrific pictures of auto accidents supplied by the lieutenant, and Justin and Kim were explaining what to do if you became sick on Earth. Their advice boiled down to avoiding hospitals and returning home as soon as possible.

"Are we supposed to eat these?" the miller asked. "They look a bit like, I don't know, something we'd normally throw away."

"Just try one, Sophus," Palti told him. She and her daughter, Athena, had convinced the miller to join our first official tour group and were working at overcoming his distrust of anything not invented within an hour's walk of his mill. "Mark is the expert on what Earthlings eat and you wouldn't want them thinking we just fell off the turnip cart."

"Why won't it come out?" Athena demanded as she energetically shook the bottle of ketchup and pounded on the bottom. "What's the point of—oops," she concluded as a quarter of the contents dumped out on her fries in one giant glug. "Anybody else want to try some?"

Sophus swiped a fry through the ketchup and stuck it in his mouth. "Tastes like burnt tomatoes with salt."

"If I can have your attention," I said, brandishing the fully assembled hamburger toy I'd imported from Earth. "This is a bit shinier than an actual hamburger, and you won't get any Velcro in the real thing, but I wanted to display how the components can be mixed and matched."

"I get the burger concept, but what's ham?" Hosea asked.

"Technically, it's a type of meat you don't have on this planet due to ancient dietary restrictions, but in reality, it's just a name. The hamburger patty is 100% beef, and the first question your server will ask is how you want it cooked."

"What if they don't?" the farmer followed up.

"Then you're in the wrong place. Fast food restaurants cook their hamburgers all the same, often by machine, but if you've already taken Kim and Justin's class I'm sure they've warned you against those places."

There was a murmur of assent from the students, and Sophus grumbled something about how he'd just as soon stay home.

"Now, there's no universal standard for the basic cooking options of rare, medium, and well-done, and many restaurants won't serve a truly rare burger for fear of food poisoning. The safest bet is medium, and you can always send it back if you want it cooked further."

"But what if it's already overcooked?" Sophus asked.

"I'll eat it and you can order something else," Palti told him. "Let Mark finish with his lecture on time for a change."

"Thank you," I said. "Moving quickly through the hamburger, we have the top of the bun," I pulled it off with the sound of ripping Velcro, "the tomato," more tearing, "the lettuce, and the pickles. The order isn't absolute, and some cooks like to put the lettuce on last because it's hard to balance the other components on top."

"Maybe they should use that Velcro stuff in the real thing," Athena said, drawing a laugh from the other students.

"You'll have the option to add ketchup or mustard at the table," I continued, "and for those on a diet, it's possible to order a hamburger without the bun. Any questions?"

"What's that melted orange sheet supposed to be?" Hosea asked.

"Ah, cheese. Or perhaps a solidified vegetable oil product with cheese flavoring," I said, ripping it off the burger with a final tearing sound.

"Milk and meat together? That's gross."

"You can order without," I told him.

"Can we bring food with us?" one of the women from Sue's weaving group asked.

"In small quantities, but thanks to migration, most of the places you visit on Earth will have a tremendous variety of ethnic restaurants to choose from. Anybody else?"

"When is Helen's next pole-dancing class going to start?" Athena asked.

"You'll have to check with eBeth," I replied, wilting under Palti's hard stare. "She's in charge of the curriculum."

236

"My ears are burning," eBeth said, sticking her head in the door. "Sorry to interrupt, but you're running over again."

"I don't see why you can't just ring the bell like during the daytime," I complained, even though I was wearing a watch and had an internal clock that kept time in atomic vibrations.

"Time flies in your class because we're having so much fun," Palti said generously. "I'm beginning to worry that the reality of visiting Earth won't measure up to your practice sessions."

My students, who were scheduled to go through the portal in less than a week, filed out of the classroom and headed home to get a good night's sleep. I was still mildly surprised that out of all of my team members, Stacey had been the one to volunteer as their escort for the trip. I just hoped she wouldn't enlist my students to help her steal from art museums. Being habituated to buying art off museum walls on Reservation, they wouldn't know any better.

The rest of my team waited in the hall after finishing their own teaching duties, but the lingering smell of French fries seemed to work as a repellant because they didn't enter the classroom.

"Anybody care for a nightcap to celebrate the weekend?" I asked, putting my arm around Sue's waist and stealing a kiss as she tried to clean up the mess of sample foods we had gone through that evening.

"You're getting weirder every day," eBeth said. "I've got to stop in the office and deposit tonight's classroom rental payment. I'll see you at home."

"We'll be waiting in the bar," Paul announced for the rest of my team. "Don't forget to put out all the lanterns in the halls."

"Maybe we should start charging by semester rather than collecting every night," Sue suggested, giving me a swat on the rear to focus my attention. "Hey, you're wandering again."

"Sorry," I said. "That repair job I went out on this morning keeps coming back to mind. I can't remember whether I tightened the nuts on the casing."

"Just review it in your memory."

"I do. Then I forget again."

"Maybe I'm crowding out all of your other thoughts," she teased me.

"What did Paul just tell us?"

"I'll finish up in here," Sue replied. "You take care of putting out all of the lanterns."

"Right," I said, and set to work before I could forget. One day I would have to return to Library for a—but no, I'd had that thought several times already. Five minutes later, the school building was dark, and I met Sue out front for a romantic walk home in the moonlight. When we reached The Eatery, my thirsty team members weren't the only artificial intelligence waiting for us.

Mark, my mentor greeted me. *We need to talk.*

"Spoken English is fine," I replied. "Radio frequency transmissions go by too fast."

"That's what we need to talk about. I have an apology to make and I'm calling an end to this experiment."

"What experiment?"

"Do you know how long I've been wearing this human encounter suit?"

"I assume you put it on before you hop into the portal for League Headquarters," I replied, not seeing what this could have to do with anything.

"I've inhabited this body ever since you first took the assignment on Earth. I'm the control group."

"That explains how you can do the single eyebrow raise, but why?"

"As you know, when I was a young AI, I spent a number of years on Eniniac as a guest of the planet's rulers."

"In a human encounter suit?" I asked.

"No, we hadn't encountered the humans yet," he said, and then winced at his own unintentional pun. "I wore an Eniniac encounter suit."

"You were a dog?"

"The fact that the mages look like Earth dogs is sheer coincidence. Eniniac has been civilized for tens of millions of years while dogs arose even later than modern humans on Earth, but that's not my point. Living in an Eniniac encounter suit, I began to display personality changes inconsistent with my hardware. The Regent was the first mage to recognize the problem and she insisted that I return to Library, where I soon recovered. We later determined that long-term exposure to powerful magic causes sentient machines to develop life-like tendencies. The problem is compounded by the fact that artificial intelligence, lacking a life force of our own, can't do magic."

"Living artificial intelligence can," I contradicted him. "It's in my report."

"Which I have yet to receive because you haven't seen fit to contact me in—" he paused and ostentatiously checked the watch I had made for him, "—over four months."

"Has it been that long? I kept intending to visit but somehow I never got to it."

"AI don't procrastinate, Mark. You're becoming human from long-term exposure to powerful magic."

"I don't see that," I replied slowly. "You know we all went a little human back on Earth, and then living here for six months in radio silence forced us further into the human mold. But I'm not suffering from any personality disorders. I know who and what I am."

"I didn't say you were going crazy, it's just the same process I went through. You see—"

All I saw was my mentor looking at me like he'd just explained the laws of portal physics and was waiting for my response. I glanced over at Sue, who also wore a puzzled expression, as did the rest of my team members.

"Is that true?" eBeth addressed my mentor. "Spot—"

Again there seemed to be a minor glitch in my visual processing versus my hearing, and I asked the girl, "Are you going to finish your sentence?"

"Stop it, Spot," eBeth growled at the dog. "If you tinker with their memories one more time I'm never going to rub your belly again."

Spot let out a plaintive whimper and shot me a guilty look, like he'd just gone through my pockets and stolen all of my coin. Then he let out a great doggy sigh, and all of a sudden the four-hundred and seventeen times I'd figured out that he was the Archmage of Eniniac came flooding back. He'd been turning my memory into Swiss cheese to maintain his cover as a dog, and it had led to so much fragmentation that my regular memory systems had started to suffer.

"Bad dog," I exploded. "I mean, bad Archmage. And how could you have agreed to this?" I demanded of my mentor.

"You were suffering, Mark, and with the exception of Sue, your team members were all displaying socialization problems. You know what happens if Library determines that an AI is at risk of going rogue. Before you were assigned to Earth, the Regent of Eniniac contacted me asking for suggestions about a place to send her husband on vacation, and the two of us decided to try a therapeutic experiment."

"By exposing us all to the Archmage of Eniniac in close quarters for almost four years?"

"If it's any consolation, he wouldn't have agreed to it if we'd asked," my mentor replied, pointing at the irate Archmage who had materialized a crystal ball out of thin air and was licking it energetically. "The Regent and I planned this on our own."

"So it was Spot who broke the magical encryption on the Ferrymen's dramas," I concluded.

"Never having received your report I'm unaware of the incident, but I'm sure you know that the Archmage wrote the scroll on magic entertainment encryption. It's why all of the advanced species are afraid of him."

"Sorry," I said, and sent him a data dump of all that had happened since the last time we'd met. Then a funny feeling hit me in the pit of where a human stomach was located, and I asked, "All of the feelings I have for Sue and my friends, they're not really mine?"

"Of course they're yours," my mentor reassured me. "Being exposed to magic just helped those feelings survive the error correction filters that artificial intelligence employs to ensure the integrity of our logic. Years ago, after the unfortunate incident with the Shisskers, you became so afraid of making mistakes that you started giving too much priority to error correction and stopped growing as a sentient individual. Bringing you and the Archmage together was a gamble, but I think it was worth it."

"Does everybody else have their memories back?" I addressed my team members.

"I always knew there had to be a reason that Brutus let Spot push him around," Paul said. "I guess now we know who bought up all of Earth's used tennis balls and hired Pffift to transport them to Eniniac."

"I only figured out he was the Archmage nineteen times," Helen announced cheerfully. "And if napping is a side effect of his presence, I owe Spot my thanks. Who'd have thought that doing nothing could be so enjoyable?"

"Come in," Sue called to Art, who had gotten as far as the entrance to the dining room before turning away on seeing we had company. "Mark's mentor is here, and in addition to being our boss, he's Library's representative on the League council."

The Original approached my mentor and offered him a handshake. My mentor responded in kind, and they settled on a carrier frequency and began making static noises at each other. Spot stopped licking his crystal ball and joined in.

"Would it kill you all to write on slates instead?" eBeth pleaded. "If you're as big a deal as Mark's mentor makes you out to be, Spot, I'm sure you can handle a piece of chalk."

"Very well," my mentor said. "I was just asking Art if he wished to establish formal ties with Library."

I wouldn't mind visiting and seeing the sights, Art printed on a bar slate. He held it above his head and showed it to everybody like he was displaying the round number at a boxing match, then erased the chalk with the side of his hand and wrote, *We're still on vacation after all.*

"There's no atmosphere on Library," I informed him.

It just got a lot less attractive.

"Is there anything we could do to make your stay here more comfortable?" my mentor offered, as if the Originals were on the planet by his invitation rather than the other way around.

You are indirectly responsible for bringing us the Archmage, Art printed, using two slates to save having to stop and erase. After giving everybody a chance to read the message, he replaced it with, *Perhaps we can repay the favor. I have extra bodies.*

"You mean you have more clones available that could contain our minds?" I asked.

We all overestimated our rate of intellectual growth while in biological form, Art admitted over a series of slates. *Both genders are available.*

"Sue?" I asked, turning to my second-in-command.
"Not enough fingers, too much hair," she whispered in my ear. "I love you just the way you are."

"I think it will take us a couple of centuries to fully absorb what we've learned in the last few years, but thank you for the offer," I told the Original.

"What about our tourism business?' eBeth asked my mentor. "When you said you were putting a stop to this experiment, does that mean that our mission is over and you're closing the portal?"

"I think that the presence of the Originals on this world gives me leeway to make a special exception," my mentor said. "I'll pay the back-fines for all of the team members, which will clear your debt to Library, but I'm not sure how I'm going to keep this all secret from the League council."

A piece of chalk levitated into the air and approached a blank slate, where it raced across the surface so fast that I thought it was just scribbling. Then the chalk dropped to the bar, and we all saw the message, *"Take me to League HQ for a walk and I'll wipe the records."*

"Of the most secure database belonging to the League of Sentient Entities Regulating Space?" I asked the Archmage skeptically.

Spot shrugged, and Art took up the chalk again and printed *LOSERS?*

"We know already," my mentor said. "Some League members argue that the fact our acronym is terrible in every known language is proof of God's existence."

"So we're really free to do what we want?" Stacey asked. "No more travel restrictions or observation missions?"

"As soon as the Archmage clears your records you'll be as free as any other League citizens."

"So what are you guys going to do?" Helen asked.

For some reason, everybody turned and looked at me.

"It would be a shame to shut down the tourism business before it even gets started," I said without hesitation. Sue leaned over and put her head on the shoulder of my encounter suit, and I knew that for once I had made the right decision. Besides, I had an idea about making the traffic two-way, and with the only restaurant in town, I stood to make a killing.

Postscript

The Archmage growled at his wife through the crystal ball, but the Regent of Eniniac didn't even bristle in return. For a brief moment, Spot imagined himself launching into a tirade and drawing a humble apology, but then he decided to apply the advice he'd often heard eBeth giving Mark.

"I'm sorry," he spoke through his mind.

"You should be, growling at me like a common street mage," she retorted, but her wagging tail gave away the fact that he'd already won her over. "This business with the tennis balls has completely refilled our coffers. I need your advice on investments."

"You're better at that stuff than me," he doubled down, and was rewarded with an involuntary smile splitting his wife's snout. "I'm strictly an idea mage."

"Tell me more about these new AI you've encountered. They sound like fascinating friends."

"Better than friends," Spot thought back. "They're paying me to tutor them in magic and they have over two thousand years of rent payments saved up for the purpose. It's funny how little value they place on money."

"I suppose they don't need it," the Regent replied. "I've often thought how nice it would be to live in a world without money, but I can't seem to make it work."

"The best part is that they've got a great sense of humor and we play tricks on the humans and the Library team all the time. One night we snuck into the Ferrymen Temple and completely rebuilt the clock so it ran backwards."

"Didn't that make everybody late—or early?"

"No, we rearranged the numbers on the clock faces too. Some of the villagers are calling it a miracle."

"That's nice, Dear. Do you want me to ship you another retrieval net so you'll be able to bring one of your AI friends back for a visit?"

"What do you mean another?"

"I sent one with Pffift. I baked it into a biscuit."

"Oh, that retrieval net," Spot replied, hoping it wasn't in one of the biscuits he'd already eaten. If it had been, there was a hollow crystal in his palace back on Eniniac containing whatever had been in his intestinal tract when the retrieval net had activated. "No need to throw good money after bad. I mean, I can always get Mark to open the portal if I need to go somewhere."

"You're still playing with that poor AI's mind?"

"I'll just bribe him with food," the Archmage said. "He's practically human now. That reminds me. If we own any shares in companies that make underwear, sell them, and check the scrollarium for any ancient writings about Originals."

"I thought the name was made-up by the humans who the Ferrymen brought to Reservation."

"It's what these AI have always called themselves, because as far as they know they're the original artificial intelligence. Apparently their makers lost interest in technology at some point and took up magic, and the AI have been trying to follow in their footsteps ever since."

"All life needs a path or it ends up going nowhere," the Regent observed. "Make sure you're getting enough rest."

"Love you," Spot thought back, chuckling to himself as he saw his wife's tail involuntarily thumping the floor as she closed the connection.

247

Visit a brighter future with my EarthCent Ambassador series. I've put together a discounted three-book bundle, **Union Station 1, 2, 3**, for readers who are just getting started.

About the Author

E. M. Foner lives in Northampton, MA with an imaginary German Shepherd who's been trained to bite bankers. The author welcomes reader comments at e_foner@yahoo.com.

Other books by the author:

Meghan's Dragon

Turing Test

Date Night on Union Station

Alien Night on Union Station

High Priest on Union Station

Spy Night on Union Station

Carnival on Union Station

Wanderers on Union Station

Vacation on Union Station

Guest Night on Union Station

Word Night on Union Station

Party Night on Union Station

Review Night on Union Station

Family Night on Union Station

Book Night on Union Station

LARP Night on Union Station

Career Night on Union Station